Probability

ANTHONY HUEY

NEWMAN SPRINGS PUBLISHING
320 Broad Street
Red Bank, NJ 07701

First originally published by Newman Springs Publishing 2024

ISBN 979-8-89061-134-5 (Paperback)
ISBN 979-8-89061-206-9 (Hardcover)
ISBN 979-8-89061-135-2 (Digital)

Printed in the United States of America

To S-D-S. I ride for you 4ever.

CHAPTER 1

2005

S he always hated the condescending way the caseworker looked at her. If there was any other way that she could get the help she needed, she would've done it already. Friends told her this was the system they put them in. There was only a few more months left, and she knew that with her aspirations, she could get her two-year degree and a better way of life for herself and her son.

As Trish walked down the city blocks of the downtown office district, having just left the scrutiny of the child support agency, she remained steadfast as she struggled to keep control of her emotions. But she was human and getting your heart broken is not an easy fix.

He'd told her he loved her, and since no one had ever said that to her before with such sincerity, she fell for it and gave up the most sacred part of herself. He'd seemed like a good person, even though he did not go to church like she did or even share the same religion. However, he'd seemed well-versed in the Word, and that made an impression on her.

Her mother objected to her being with him; she said she had seen it before—his swag, his demeanor, his reputation of being a go-getter while being a foreign exchange student at her daughter's high school. It mirrored her own experience with Trish's father. He was a smooth talker too, and dealing with him caused her to be a teen mother, raising a child with a deadbeat for a father. So when Trish

1

approached her to tell her that the boy that she warned her about got her pregnant, all she could do was reflect on her mistakes and lash out.

She flew off the handle. She yelled, screamed, punched, and kicked at Trish, screaming at the top of her lungs, stating that she'd ruined her life, all the while cursing herself for having such a stupid daughter who followed the same mistake she made. She told her how just like her, all her plans and dreams would be ruined by having a baby and that she would never be anything than just a baby mama, just like her.

The words stung fiercely to Trish, especially coming from her mother, whom she needed the most. Their squabbling ended with her mother kicking her out the house. She told her to go and never come back especially with her damn baby. Trish had to find refuge with some of her trusted friends.

But the biggest blow was not her mother kicking her out because she was pregnant but rather a phone call she received from a girl claiming that they both were pregnant by the same guy around the same time. She confronted her boyfriend to hear what he had to say about the claim when, to her desolate heartbreak, he admitted that not only was the claim true that he impregnated two girls at the same time, but he also had other children which he never told her about.

She could have crumbled into a ball of sadness and despair, broken and tainted from the world that was always going to be against her. She was going to make it; she would be the one to defy the odds. She was not going to continue the cycle and wind up bitter, jaded, and evil like her mother had become. She would still finish her education and soon enroll in college so that she could make a better life for her and her unborn son.

Who cared if his father wanted nothing to do with him? She was young and pretty and smart. There was a man out there who would appreciate her and her son, but that could wait. Her focus would be her little boy and making a life suitable for both. She loved her prince and hadn't even seen his face yet, but she knew that she would move heaven and hell to protect him.

That was the thought in her mind when that first happened more than two years ago as she walked with her little boy by her side, holding his hand as they walked down the street around the busy city. Their bus was coming soon, but there was no need to rush. Her young son had become adept at walking, and she loved every second of watching his little legs take their strides. He validated all the hard work that she had put in from graduating to finding a job and getting a small efficiency for the two of them to live in. Watching her strong little boy gave her confirmation that nothing was going to get in their way.

Her son's name was Nahshon. The father gave him that name. She liked the sound of it, plus it had a pleasing sound to her when she would say his name. She knew that he was destined for great things, and it would be her crowning achievement to sit back and watch the commencement speeches, the valedictorian speeches, and the wedding proposals.

She couldn't wait to be in attendance to witness those from her son. She could hardly wait for these benchmarks to happen and to modestly sit back for a job well done. But for now, it was the two of them, and they were going to make it the best way they could.

To lift her spirits, she began singing her favorite song to cheer her up whenever she needed some encouragement:

> *I'm the ruler of my destiny*
> *If I fall then it's because of me*
> *There is nobody who's got the power*
> *To determine what becomes of me*
> *I'm aware of what we're here to do*
> *And, do is our only choice*
> *And if you like it'll be ME and YOU*

Trish emphasized the "me and you" as she made sure her child saw her pointing at him as she said "you." It was a familiar-sounding tune to the child, and it induced a smile from him because it always made his mother react with a smile.

As they started to approach the corner of an intersection, the little boy's eyes began shifting back and forth as he clutched his mother's hand. There were floating masses of red and green blotches all around which drew his attention. As the little boy watched the blobs of color, the red blotches began to connect as if taking shape into a sinister form. The little boy stopped as it drew his attention, and he became afraid to walk toward the illuminating red color.

"Nahshon? What's the matter baby?" Trish asked her little boy.

The child halted in his steps. As his young eyes looked ahead, he saw that the frightening masses of red color forming before him. He looked up as he noticed the blotches of green float over his head and behind him and his mother.

As this was happening, a young businessman in a suit was walking along the same sidewalk and passed by Trish. He noticed the beauty of the young mother. It briefly caught his attention as he walked by. He smiled at Trish, taken by her beauty, and she returned a slight smile back at him. Then her attention shifted back to her frightened son.

"What's wrong, son? Are you afraid of the cars in the street? I won't let them get you," she assured her son.

The little boy looked up at his mother's loving face. It was the only face he'd known, and with her soft eyes, the panic eased down and the menacing color went away. The force that stopped him in his tracks melted away, and he was ready for his mother to continue guiding him along.

Seeing that her son was calm and ready to walk, Trish prepared to take her step from the corner. As she stepped off the curb, a metro bus came barreling down and plowed into her. The force of the bus knocked Nahshon a step back as blood splattered across his face and body. The driver of the bus slammed his brakes, causing the metro bus to stop halfway in the middle of the intersection.

"*Jesus!*" yelled the young man as he watched the incident unfold.

The businessman that caught his mother's attention witnessed the whole incident unfold and rushed to grab the young child from the curb. Other people along the busy street who witnessed the tragedy also ran toward the little boy.

The poor little child's face looked catatonic as he stood there unmoving as grown strangers gathered, comforting him as blotches of the color red shifted and flashed all around him in his sight while his loving mother lay mangled to death beneath a bus in the middle of the street.

CHAPTER 2

Now

He leaned back in the chair as the makeup artists loomed over him, constantly patting down the contours of his face. He was reminded over and over again to look straight ahead, but the madness surrounding him as production and set design ran about was like a magnet for his eyes.

The chaotic hustle and bustle of the backroom on talk show sets were starting to become commonplace for the renowned child psychologist and sudden media darling, Ellis Daniels. Within a year of deciding to offer himself as an expert panelist regarding children and young adult discussions, usually pitted against another panelist with opposing views, his unique style of analytical yet bluntly direct commentary had caught the media world on fire and became the downfall of whoever was arguing against him.

The moments in the discussion when Daniels had his adversary pigeonholed in a debate became so popular with millennials that video clips began going viral, sometimes added with hip-hop music and comedic special effects. He was gaining an unexpected fan base for something he felt in his heart was his calling, dispelling unfounded myths and perceptions regarding child mental issues. Social media dubbed him "Uncle Dan."

Reaching the opening that led to the main stage, he could see the empty seat that he was supposed to sit in next to the moderator of the show. The show would also be joined in discussion via remote by Francis Harlow, a well-known and very incendiary political pundit who also served as a lightning rod for conservative views upon education.

Over the last few years, there had been many controversies surrounding some of his comments on inner-city children, mainly African American and Latino children, and their lack of discipline and structure of the home. Some of his comments were looked upon as considerably racist and, in one incident, led to on studio altercation between a black educational expert and himself, in which the gentleman nearly physically attacked him for his words. Even though both gentlemen happened to be white, the studio producer thought it would be best to keep him at a distance in case the discussion got lively.

Ellis had received a heads-up on who the other guest was and conducted some reading about him the previous night. He knew that this man was a prideful person who beforehand had taken great relish in setting up the emotional traps for the people he engaged in arguments with. In fact, one such verbal entrapment led to the person issuing a threat, which he, in turn, was able to make lucrative through a lawsuit on the grounds that he was having his life threatened.

"Now they want to be cordial with Mr. Harlow and mainly listen to some of his points before you interject. They want to reel in the viewers' interests at some of his claims before they hear from you. Basically, they're looking for him to create controversy and future heat for future shows," said Cash, the production assistant who had been walking alongside Ellis during his stroll on to the stage area.

"So sit back and let him spew whatever misinformation and filth he prepared for show?" asked Ellis.

"No, not exactly. You...uh...well, yeah...I guess so, Dr. Daniels," Cash responded.

"Okay," said Ellis.

Ellis looked at the mannerisms and expressions of the moderator's face as his mind painted a profile of the type of person that he would be speaking to. The executive producer made a gesture that a commercial break was coming, and the signals were given out so that they could get ready for break. It was now time for Ellis to step on stage and takes his seat for the next segment.

"Now remember, look natural and go with what the producers wanted."

"I don't care about that…"

"Well, we do. We have people from our media team monitoring social media outlets to see what the reaction is going to be from this."

"I don't care about that either," Ellis said as he stepped past the assistant to take his walk along stage.

Ellis took his seat next to the moderator and host of the show, Joe Cumberland. As production hands positioned the Lavalier microphone on, Ellis Cumberland leaned over to whisper to him. Ellis looked back and noticed that the background in the distance was different than that of Cumberland. It was a camera trick used to give off the illusion of being elsewhere instead of next to him. Also, it eliminated the illusion that the two of them will be in the same space to go against the other commentator zooming in.

"I'm very excited about this. You two are going to do great. They explained to you how this is going to go?"

"More for less," responded Ellis.

"Just let him sound off what he has to say and then you can go on with your opinion, and the rest will work itself out," added Cumberland.

All production people scurried off the stage, and the count-down to airing began. On the lead cameras the intro graphics came on, and the music could be heard in the studio as the show opened. Ellis, now becoming accustomed with the media appearances, began to straighten his facial expression and look straight ahead for the camera. And so the show began.

"Welcome back to hour number 2 of *The Cumberland Experience*. In this segment, we are joined by Francis Harlow, national director of outreach media for Help Our Children Now, the rising lobbyist group that is making waves along the political spectrum advocating for systematic changes in not only the home life of children but the learned curriculum being used in schools. They have recently come under fire for comments made regarding historical reference material and its effect on different races of children. Also joining me today is Dr. Ellis Daniels, assistant director of the Brooks Institute for Child Wellness and a leading advocate for at-risk children and their circumstances. Thank you both for joining me today, gentlemen."

"Thank you, sir."

"Great to be here."

"Director Harlow, I would like to start with you, sir. How are you doing today?"

"I am great, but let me start off by correcting something here. Help Our Children Now is *not* a lobbyist group. We are a rising momentum organization that is dedicated and necessary in the struggle against the onslaught of damaging trauma to children and youth by propaganda in school and the ascension of social media. The same type of social media that has made an instant star out of the gentleman joining us today," answered Harlow.

There was a hush in the studio as production crew members were taken aback by the immediate attack on Daniels from Harlow. Meanwhile, Ellis remained unshakably calm as his analytical mind began to kick in while he looked at Harlow's facial expression:

- His eyebrow above his left eye lifted. He was proud about what he said.
- He was slightly disappointed by my lack of reaction. He expected more.
- He is a compulsive liar and denier of truth. He doesn't handle facts well.

Momentarily stunned by Harlow's initial statement, Cumberland acted to rebound and reinstate control over his own show.

"Let's keep it cordial here, gentlemen. Now, Director Harlow, you said in your initial statement about propaganda in schools. Can you expand more on what the meaning of that is and what effect it has on the mental state of youth and children today?" asked Cumberland.

"Of course. I meant no disrespect to the other guy here. Listen, I understand history, I respect history, but if there is something that's historically damaging in the now for children to have to read about and learn, I am not for it…and neither is my organization. You have enough to worry about these days with the rise in violence, drugs problems in the home, and as I stated before, the media, especially social media.

"Atrocities in history are bad. We all know that, but should they be force-feeding it to our children's psyches so that they can feel bad about something they weren't responsible for? I don't think so. And see, that is the problem with modern-day liberalism. It creates in society a segment of the population that is guilt ridden over things they couldn't control and unleash them and their stigmas into the adult world, where even more violent acts can take place.

"What, as a society, are we going to have if all we do is trauma-tize our children with built-in traumas that will only translate into abstract and violent behavior? I don't get it. I don't get it!" Harlow responded as he gestured his hands in confusion.

"Now wait a minute. You are obviously referring to white children, excuse me, Caucasian children? You can't possibly be green-lighting the idea that's been going around politically of omitting historical atrocities done to other races by individuals considered Caucasian? Because you know there is a growing debate on actually not teaching the effects of African American slavery as well as the Jewish Holocaust. You're actually talking about rewriting history books?"

"And why not? What good does it do now to create an already established racial divide by placing blame on a generation that has zero responsibility for what occurred in history, which, by the way, doesn't even matter in the here and now," responded Harlow.

"I'm sorry, viewers. I'm at a loss with this guy," said Cumberland.

Ellis sat there with the same unchanged expression, taking in the reaction and movements of both men speaking. *This has gone far enough. Time to challenge his ego on with an expression.*

Ellis slowly introduced a jovial smirk on his face. From wherever he was viewing the interview, Harlow immediately noticed Ellis and went on the attack.

"I'm sorry, did I say something humorous to the 'TikTok doctor' in this interview? I've been waiting to hear what little you have to add to this conversation."

"Well, not much. I'm still stuck wondering where the application of *help* is that's in your company's name?" Ellis responded, sounding puzzled.

The response by Ellis stopped Harlow and Cumberland dead in their tracks, but Harlow was a veteran in shock media, and he would not be undone. He struggled to smother the quiet rage inside him so that he could center on Ellis in front of the viewers.

"Listen, I did not come on this platform to assault anyone or seek conflict among two obviously intelligent men. Mr. Daniels, I did not mean to offend you. I know that this is a rough period in your life and your family, so I can understand if you don't fully get the message that my organization is trying to convey in the best interest of our children."

Ellis's face returned from a smirk back to a nonemotionally stoic stare. *He's researched on me and is trying to get personal. Time to shut him down.*

"Director Harlow, *The Cumberland Experience* is not the type of vehicle for—"

"The problem, Harlow, is *you*. Not once in this…whatever you want to call this…have you spoken anything about mental health solutions, solutions for children who are experiencing legitimate and documented psychological problems. That is what I do. Politics is what you are. Politics is what you do. The two do not need to meet. You have got a lot of nerve coming on here to push your agenda. Before you answer, 'What agenda?' I will tell you. You are well documented, sir, and some of your unpopular views among race, particularly African American and Latino, is extensive, so much so that there happens to be footage of you that you and your organization have tried extremely hard to bury at a luncheon given by the Sons of Freedom, a well-known white supremacist group that honored you with an award at their event. I know that the footage is graphic. Some of the things that the audience said are not for the viewing public's ears. But I will say that your speech about 'lifting up our white children back on top and putting those black and browns back under their heel' would make good reference to who you are.

"I haven't cleared it with the producers here to air that seven-and-a-half-minute footage, but I have provided them a link which they can put on the screen now for the viewing public to look it up.

"You should be careful, Mr. Harlow, about the media because anything that you said can be used against you. The Internet is unrelenting, and if it comes out your mouth, you and your agendas are fair game. I am for the children, and I will not be back on the show. Cumberland, this guy is trash," Ellis said as he stood up and took off the Lavalier microphone off his lapel to put on the counter while he walked off stage. The production assistant walked up to him in a hurried frenzy.

"Where are you going? This segment isn't over!"

"It's over for me," Ellis replied.

Another one of the production's media guys approached Ellis in the corridor, staring down at the tablet in his hand.

"This is phenomenal! Within the last nine minutes, the exchange between you and Harlow went viral. The first viral clip to air was titled 'Uncle Dan shuts down racist within seconds!' The link you gave has gone viral too! You've become a hit!"

"I don't care. All I care about is the work. I have somewhere else to be," responded Ellis as he left the scene of backstage confusion on the production set. Cumberland and his producers would have to insert a new segment without him.

CHAPTER 3

E llis's fingers ran across the groove of the wet stone surface. His fingers went along the lines of the edge, tracing the indents that made up the letters of his young son's name. He remembered the first day he looked at him, so tiny, his eyes on them as they took great pride. That glorious day played over in his mind as his fingers went over the date that he was born. He remembered so much love in that room as both grandmothers stood there, doing their coaching. He was standing beside his wife, encouraging her as she strained her breath and pushed her child into the world. He was so excited and anxious to meet his son, something that he always wanted his whole life. In just a few minutes, it became reality.

The nurse handed Ellis his newborn son, and as he looked, he made an unspoken promise to himself and God to never leave him and always protect him. Immediately he brought the baby to his wife, and the three embraced as tears ran down both their eyes. One of the grandmothers took a picture of the three and hugged the other grandmother in the room. He and his wife, Dana, took turns kissing on their newborn son and then they suddenly looked at each other and made a silent whisper to each other of "I love you."

This blissful image flowed through his mind as if it was occurring all over again, and it was pure joy to feel it. He was feeling the letters and numbers that spelled the day his son, Grant, was born.

And then his fingers felt the grooves in the stone that spelled the day his ten-year-old pride and joy died.

Tears raced down his face as he retracted his hand as if the stone was suddenly poisonous. The full weight of grief and mourning returned to him as the blissful thoughts of his son were replaced by images from the saddest, most horrific day of his life. The feeling forced Ellis to his knees as he lamented as he did every time he came to the cemetery since the burial of his only child nearly four years ago.

As he struggled to keep his composure without breaking down, he felt a hand rest on the shoulder.

"Hello, El…"

Ellis turned to see who was behind him, and it was Adrian, his former brother-in-law and one of the few people in his former wife's family that never turned their back on him. Now in his twenties and a first-year med student, Adrian had grown up idolizing his older brother-in-law and sympathized with the anguish and pain Ellis was experiencing along with his sister.

"Amazing. Every time I look at you, I still see the little boy who was quick to hand me his player 2 controller to join him at gaming while his sister was helping his mom cook Thanksgiving dinner. And now…you're a man. I'm so proud of you, Adrian," Ellis said as he welcomed the sight of the young man.

"Don't forget, you were the one who taught me how to drive when I was fifteen. And prom? You were the one who sponsored the hotel room for me and my friends to take our prom dates, and you didn't even tell my sister! You will always be a big brother to me," Adrian said in gratitude.

"Yeah," responded Ellis.

"And apparently the Internet feels the same way, brother, or should I say 'Unc'?" Adrian joked.

"Oh yeah…that. Jeez, that's so embarrassing," Ellis responded as they both chuckled.

The two men stopped laughing at each other and turned their attention to the grave in front of them. Ellis stared intensely at the soil covering the area where his son's coffin lay underground.

"He's down there. Grant's down there…"

"I know, brother. I know," Adrian replied.

"My son…my son…," Ellis said as the grief began to overtake him.

Adrian went to place his hand on Ellis's shoulder but was suddenly interrupted by the flashing of the bright lights by the car down the hill parked in the distance.

"Hey, El, I'm sorry to come up here and disrupt you like this. It's just that my sister is in the car, and she won't come out until you leave. If you need more time, I can go back and let her know that we can come back a little later."

"Adrian, it's okay. I don't want to hold you guys up, and I think I'm good for today. Please let your sister know I'm leaving now," Ellis replied in a melancholy tone.

"Okay. Thanks, brother," Adrian said as he walked back down toward his car.

Following the tragic death of their son, Ellis and Dana struggled to go on in their marriage, but the weight of it and the fact that Dana blamed Ellis for their son's death only made their division escalate, and it eventually caused them to divorce. It had been almost two years since the divorce, and she still would not speak to him. Some of the other relatives followed suit as well; such is the nature of divorce.

Adrian, on the other hand, did not share the same views as his family and still maintained his relationship with Ellis. He understood that there were two people that shared the tragic loss and did not look at it in the narrow view that some of the relatives had who only saw the loss from Dana's point of view. It didn't exactly make him the favored person in the family, but at least any messages that needed to be given to Ellis, he would be the designated one to give them since they were still cordial.

Before Adrian got all the way downhill toward his car, Ellis stood upright while straightening out his jacket and wiping the remaining tears from his eyes and then yelled out to him, "Adrian! You tell Dana I lost my son too!"

"I know, brother. I know," replied Adrian as he turned back around and made his way to the car.

Ellis watched the car and his former wife in the passenger seat as she obviously was putting up an effort to not look at him. For a split second, she turned her head, and he could see the pain and anguish on her face peppered with the expression of anger and resentment that she now felt for him. He began to wonder if she could ever look at him again.

Ellis turned back around and said his parting words to the headstone of his dead son. He kissed the stone and made one last attempt to collect the wetness in his eyes. He then started to make his way along the other side of the hill back to his car, and when he got close enough to his car, he could hear the sound of Adrian's car door opening up as his former wife was finally comfortable with coming out to see their son.

It was a sad situation for the two of them because he never stopped loving her, but love could not bring their son back. He got in his car and made his way out of the cemetery for his return home.

Ellis approached his porch, and right at the top of the steps leading to the front door was a thick manila package that he quickly recognized as the usual calling card of his friend Reed. Reed was a colleague of his at the institute and had a penchant for being a cheapskate when it came to mailing and was likely to just leave documents on people's doorsteps as opposed to paying for mailing packages.

Usually it was a case file that he wanted his input on or needed help in providing information to help close. Ellis was growing tired of giving his friend free advice just for him to reap the benefits. Though they were in different fields, he still felt like he was giving the milk for free, but no one could say that he was not a good friend.

Ellis grabbed the package and went in his door. It was cold and lifeless in his condo. He missed sounds of his ten-year-old boy running around, and even though they didn't live at that place at that time, he still missed the life that having a family brought with it. How lonely it was to come home alone.

He sat down in a kitchen chair and opened the manila folder and proceeded to empty out the contents within. There were notes, a case file, and a cassette tape. Ellis smirked because he knew that Reed knew him all too well and that he probably had a cassette player in his house. He grabbed his outdated cassette player from a shelf in the cupboard and popped the tape in while sitting back down and then pressed Play.

"Ellis, my friend. How you doing this fine evening? This is your buddy Reed. I know you have a flair for the old-school, so I put this info on a cassette tape because I know you got one…heehee. Anyway, dude, I got this case that you might be interested in, and you know me, I don't have enough brainpower to fix one case. This is a very curious case, but since I know how you have a flair for getting people to become cooperative with you and an understanding where they're coming from, I think that this would be right down your alley.

"It's a young man, almost seventeen to be exact. He's close to graduating, so he's one of them child geniuses, but he's very withdrawn and possible PTSD symptoms. He's a foster system kid, so that might be the reason, but there are other elements that are very peculiar, and I think that you can really dig to the root of it.

"Of course I do understand that you're a busy man, and I also know how hard it is for you in your bereavement process. So, Ellis, please, if you're not interested or you don't want to be involved, I more than understand. But I know how much you like to throw you yourself into your work to help deal with the grief, so you know…

"Anyway, if you're interested, take a look and just continue listening. I recorded a brief explanation of the case file for your initial information, and you can give me a call, and maybe next week I can give you more info on the case so we can go from there. Take care, buddy. I'm praying for you."

Ellis pressed down on this Stop button of the cassette player. He took a moment to reflect and ponder while trying to rid himself of the thoughts that plagued him earlier during the day at the cemetery. He started to lift the file and flung it back down on the kitchen table. Then he tapped his fingers a few times along the cassette player.

Unfortunately Reed was right. He did throw himself into his work too much. Ellis cut the overhead lights in the kitchen on, opened the case file, and pressed Play on the cassette player so that he could hear the rest of the case information.

CHAPTER 4

Ellis arrived at his office at the usual time, and as always, he looked at his doorknob to see if there were any fingerprints or smudges on them. He was very particular about who came into his office, and as a force of habit, he always checked to see if someone invaded his workspace. As he predicted, there were fingerprint smudges, which meant that somebody went there early to drop off something. Although Ellis himself never claimed to be clairvoyant, he knew exactly what it was.

So once he walked into the office, it came as no surprise to him that on his office desk were a couple of files placed down.

"Reed," he said as he took a seat in his chair.

Reed was always known for leaving just enough info to get your beak wet. He would've made a great talk-show host. When Ellis had called him and left a message telling Reed that he would view the case, he knew that he was only looking at a tidbit, just enough to make him curious. That's how Reed usually drew him in.

Ellis placed his travel bag on the desk and put out the cassette player, which still had the cassette tape that Reed had sent him. He pressed Play, so he could hear the clinical information again as he scrolled through some of the new documentation:

> *"Young client is a sixteen-year-old black male.*
> *His name is Nahshon Carpenter. He has previously*
> *been in the care of clinical psychologists Dr. Tara*

19

Billings, Dr. Thomas Moore, and Dr. Robert Rice with complicated and unsuccessful result. Young man displays no signs of neurological impairments or intellectual challenges. In fact, aptitude tests prove the young man to have staggering intuitive and reasoning capacities. Social involvement in capability skills are hampered, however, due to possible PTSD or other types of previous trauma. The young man shows signs of severe social isolation."

As he listened to Reed's assessment, Ellis ran his fingers to various pages of each previous doctor's files. They contained nothing peculiar that stood out—DSM5, ACE test scores, multiple DAF forms spanning well over a decade, ETRs, and subsequent IEPs. Nothing out of the ordinary, and they were all in one system since childhood. Ellis bypassed much of the documents and took out the therapist's notes and MEDSOM reports from each doctor's files; they usually provided him with a good start.

"My guess is you're probably going through therapist's notes and reports. You like to get to the meat of the matter. I know you too well," Reed continued as he laughed.

Ellis paused to sigh at the notion that Reed had him so figured out. Was he that transparent? He had figured it out pretty well by himself, and he knew that there had to be a hook to why Reed had brought this to his attention. He was just waiting for the big bang.

"Okay, enough preliminaries. Here's what you've been waiting for. Real X-Files stuff... Additionally, there has been detailed information from his last previous psychologists, Dr. Moore and Dr. Rice, regarding the possibility of extrasensory perception as a catalyst for his ego-syntonic isolation. Special tests conducted outside of the standard

*norm indicates Nahshon as showing abnormal signs
of possible clairvoyance and precognition abilities."*

Ellis's ears perked up at the last sentence. Finally Reed had his full attention.

*"Maybe seeing is believing, Ellis. Go ahead
and pop in the CD I made for you."*

Ellis looked down at the manila folder and noticed that it wasn't empty. There was still a wrapped CD, which he took out and stared at. He walked over to his monitor and CD player and put the CD in. He didn't return back to his seat. He leaned back to relax and used the remote to press Play.

As the video cut on, there was Nahshon, sitting alone in his chair in what was apparently Reed's new office. His head was hanging down low, and you could not see the young man's face. The view of the camera didn't show Reed on it, so obviously it was close by him, as if he was interrogating the boy as opposed to interviewing him.

*"Nahshon, how you doing since the last time
we talked, bro?"*
*"Please don't call me 'bro.' You know what my
name is."*
Sigh. "Fine. All right, let's begin…"
Click.
*"Today is May 17, 2019. Reference number
2885, case number 342811. Subject, Nahshon
Carpenter, African-American male, age 16. This is
a base interview on the young man's daily life rou-
tine as conducted by assigned psychologist, Dr. Reed
Richardson.*
*"So, Nahshon, how have you been this week?
Has there been anything of note worth sharing? The
floor is yours…"*

"No. I don't have much to say about anything."

"It's okay, Nahshon, you are in a safe place. It's my job to get to understanding more and helping you out with some of the issues you might be experiencing."

Scoff. "I don't think so."

"But I am. And I'm here to help you. I'm just looking out for your well-being."

"My 'well-being'? You don't even know me. So please, respectfully, don't hand me that crap."

"Fine."

Click.

Reed gestured with his arm up, tapping a switch showing that he turned off the recording device.

"All right, enough of this crap. So who did you get into it with, man? Who'd you get a fight with this time?"

"I was defending myself. I was attacked by a bunch of kids, and they went hard at me, so why are you getting on my back about it?"

"You got too much of a chip on your shoulder. Sometimes that could be a magnet for troublemakers."

The response that Reed gave made Nahshon recoil in his seat, as if he knew no matter what he said, Reed would be taking the attackers' side, so he hung his head low in expressed dejection. Nahshon sank back into his seat.

From the moment Nahshon began to speak, the analytical process of Ellis's mind began to kick in. Almost from the start, he noticed a conflict in aspects of the young man's personality. His vaunted deductive skills began to paint a landscape of the boy's psyche. Every little tick, every little nuance that Nahshon showed his mind compartmentalized. Even though the exchange between the young man and Reed was brief, there were questions that arose in his mind to be answered as he thought to himself:

- The boy has a relaxed posture in the seat. Even though the surrounding is uncomfortable he doesn't look nervous. Obviously Reed has made more attempts than what he says to pry into this boy.
- The way he snapped back at Reed's admonishment. Clearly he does not like him, but he fears him for what he might uncover. Uncover what? What is it about this boy that's making him so guarded and making Reed so intrusive?
- Every seven seconds, his eyes shift around to different areas, even when they appear to be looking down. What is he looking around for or at?
- Though his body language would indicate that he is guarded, it looks like a front. The boy's actually yearning for guidance, but I can't say it's of the parental type, something deeper than that. Maybe something traumatic in origin? What is he trying to control?
- He was hoping for Reed to show concern over the marks on his face from his fight but subconsciously showed disappointment at Reed's not showing interest.
- His right foot is slightly turned sixty degrees, indicating a reflex reaction of flight or fight from something he's visibly seeing. As if he's always on edge. What is it that has you so ready to always react?
- He is also fully aware that Reed is still recording him.

Ellis sat back in his chair, his interest narrowing in on the young man on the video screen. As he looked on, he could see Reed coming into view with a chair that he placed close to where Nahshon was sitting. He perched himself in the chair and leaned in at the boy as if to speak intimately to him. Ellis could see a dramatic change in Reed's expression.

"*The images, do you see them around you now, Nahshon, and are the values shifting right now?*"

"*Constantly,*" *Nahshon replied again.*

"*So is it something that you can't necessarily control, right? Then how are you able to understand them?*"

"*At first I didn't, but as I got older, I started to recognize things happen because of what I saw,*" *Nahshon replied.*

Reed eased up in the chair and put his two index fingers up against his lip as if he was pondering.

"*I think it's a good thing that we keep this between us. The medical community. The science community. I don't think they could comprehend this phenomenon that you have. Is okay to call it that?*"

"*There's nothing 'phenomenal' about it, Dr. Richardson. It's draining.*"

"*Draining?*" *Reed asked.*

"*Do you even understand what I'm saying right now? I don't think you understand how life works.*"

"*Young man, I—*"

"*No, you don't. Everything is chaos. Millions and millions of possibilities waiting to happen at any given moment,*" *Nahshon interjected.*

"*I'm sorry, but I simply don't believe that. There are calculated results to a plan. Science dictates that.*"

"*Science also dictates that every action carries a reaction, so why is it so hard to believe that every movement creates a series of different possible results?*" *Nahshon responded.*

The boy sounds quite astute. And he's correct, Ellis thought to himself.

Reed reached into his pocket and took out his small cell phone. It had been buzzing on and on since the moment he arrived at his office. He had the phone on vibrate so that whoever was calling could not interrupt them.

"So you can't control your ability?"

"I told you before I can't control it."

"Have you really tried to challenge your limits? Explore your potential?" Reed urged.

"I'm telling you it happens all the time. Why are you pushing me so much! You're no different than the rest of them, especially the ones that tried to use me!" Nahshon replied in an agitated tone.

"Nahshon, let me help. We can understand this, but I need you to trust in me. Now please, in detail, explain how this sight of yours occurs," said Reed in a soothing tone.

"I'm sorry, but I think I don't have anything else to say other than you should be very careful with that phone of yours. I don't think that brand was built to last," replied Nahshon.

"This phone? Oh, you're very mistaken. I paid a nice hunk of change for this. This model came out just last year."

Nahshon expressed a slight smirk.

"I have a colleague of mine, actually an old friend I'd like to introduce you to."

"More users."

"It's not like that. I think that together he and I can get to the bottom of how you are experiencing probabilities that you often see. If that really is the case."

"It is the case, Dr. Richardson, but right now I would be more concerned with that defective phone and finding out if it was made by the same people *that made that defective overhead camera you got in here that is still videotaping me," Nahshon replied.*

Reed sat back in his chair with a sarcastic look on his face. Just then his phone began to flicker wildly, and the touch of it became hot in his palm. He looked down and watched as it short-circuited in his hand. Angered and in disbelief, he looked back up at the young man and saw him returning a sarcastic smile of his own.

"I'll get my friend to see you next week," Reed said as he got up out the seat and stormed out of his own office, slamming the door.

Nahshon lift his head slightly from his staring-down position and turned it upward to look directly at the camera that was supposedly not videotaping him. He stared for a few seconds as if he was looking through the camera and at Ellis on the other end watching. He then cracked a smirk, and the camera began to flicker and short-circuit, almost like the phone. Then the signal was lost as if the camera turned off on its own.

Ellis took the remote and turned off his monitor. He sat there in silent disbelief at what just occurred on tape. He now held more questions in his mind that his brain could handle. Any initial deducing that he started gave way to a waterfall of more additional questions on what he had just witnessed.

Then there was a type of sadness that overcame Ellis, because as much as he wanted to convince himself that he could quit taking on special cases, this was one that he was going to be all in on with both feet forward.

CHAPTER 5

It was the early morning, and Ellis was tying his tie as he looked at himself in the mirror. There was a nervous excitement about himself for his long-awaited meeting with the young man in the case that Reed had given him. He had spent over a week prepping for his encounter, constantly studying various paranormal and unexplained psychic phenomenon case studies.

He reflected on the last moments of the video and how the technology around the boy had short-circuited. He thought about the utter failure that was Reed's approach to getting to the boy. He understood why his old colleague came to him for his aid. He knew Ellis would come with a different approach. He took the case file on Nahshon and made his way out the door.

When Ellis arrived at Reed's office, he found his former colleague there anxiously waiting for him. Ellis was excited, but he did not want it to show it. He and Reed had always had a poker-like relationship toward each other.

"I know that look…You're excited, aren't you?"

"*Intrigued* would be more like it," Ellis replied.

"Uh-huh. Well, there he is, in the interview room. So what's your plan?"

"Total autonomy…that's what we agreed on, right?"

"Okay," answered Reed.

"I mean it. From the time I walk into that interview room until the time I step out, he becomes my patient," said Ellis.

"Okay! Okay! You can't blame a guy for being nosy!" Reed replied jokingly but somewhat not.

Ellis scoffed at Reed and pressed past him to go into the interview room. He did not come for needless banter with Reed. As he went to turn the doorknob, Ellis glanced through the glass at Nahshon sitting in his chair with his head down in a melancholy state. As soon as he stepped in, the young man perked up and immediately sat up in his seat as if he could see something startling in front of him.

At the same time, Ellis took in the initial expression on the boy's face. He had been through a lot, and contrary to what Reed had told him, it was obvious Nahshon had experienced this process a lot, and it was a source of great distress to him. Ellis did not want to contribute to it, so he decided to go with a different tactic than planned.

He grabbed another chair in the room and carried it along with him, nearly dragging it. Nahshon showed a look of confusion, usually when he was being questioned in the room, the person stood directly in front of him. Ellis walked past the boy and placed the chair behind him as he sat, forcing Nahshon to curiously turn his chair around to face him, making his back turned toward the surveillance camera.

"Whoo! Boy, you must've really put it on them," Ellis said.

"Huh? Oh, my face. It was a lot more—"

"No, no…not your face, your knuckles. Looking at the pattern of all the skin you took off them. You must've been nice with your fist. Especially on a group of boys," Ellis replied.

Nahshon was taken aback by his compliment. Reed never acknowledged his knuckles during the previous session. He only harped on the damage he took on his face.

"Oh! Excuse me. I didn't introduce myself…My name is Dr. Ellis Daniels," Ellis said as he extended his hand out for a handshake.

"Nahshon Carpenter," the young man said as he shook Ellis's hand.

"I know. And I know you know that I know. Okay, now that we've got the introductions out of the way, tell me about the fight you had two weeks ago," Ellis added.

Nahshon was left confused. No one had shown such genuine acknowledgment as Ellis had, especially not Reed. Because of that, it caused Nahshon's guard to go back up.

"On second thought…let's walk outside and you can tell me. I hate rooms like this. Plus, maybe I can share a thing or two about fighting that I picked up along the way."

Both confused and intrigued, Nahshon got out of his seat and followed Ellis toward the door to leave the interview room. As they made a beeline past Reed, Ellis turned toward him and placed his hand on his shoulder.

"We're going to step out for a few minutes. We'll be right back," Ellis uttered nonchalantly.

Reed was left somewhat flustered by the cavalier way Ellis had passed by with his patient, but he kept silent because of his need for Ellis's approach. As the two exited the facility, Reed looked on from the window as the two walked around the grounds. He could see Ellis talking as Nahshon followed his words intently. The gestures that Ellis was conveying looked like he was showing him some kind of fighting stance and ways of boxing.

He then gestured to the young man to mimic his moves as if giving instruction. Then the two went to motions as if mocking a sparring session, chatting with each other along the way. They stopped by one of the benches outside and took a seat. Ellis then appeared to be offering some advice that Nahshon was obviously receptive to. After a few minutes of chatting between the two, they got up and walked their way back into the facility's side door. They chuckled as they walked down the hallway returning to a waiting Reed.

"Aw, man. This is a good guy right here. It was good to meet you, Nahshon Carpenter. You got my card that I gave you outside. Use it. Give me a call anytime you want to just chat, got it?"

"Absolutely! And thanks…for everything," Nahshon replied.

"He's all yours," Ellis said as he turned toward Reed.

"We don't have to continue the session in the interview room, do we?" Nahshon asked Reed.

"Nope. In fact, we can call it a day. Here take this. It's my key to your locker. Go ahead and get your bag and stuff you had locked away. Bring the key back and I'll give you a lift back to your group home," Reed replied as he handed Nahshon his keys.

As the young man strode down the corridor, Reed turned around to face Ellis. A Cheshire cat smile was on his face.

"Well, you certainly made an impression. So what did you talk about?"

"Uh-uh. Remember the terms of our agreement," Ellis responded.

"I know, I know. But you should remember the reason why I asked for your assistance."

"Reed, I do. And I will. But it's going to take a little time, and I'm gonna have to see this kid somewhere else on the outside. That interview room is a blatant deterrent for him opening up, and you're going to get nowhere as long as he continues sitting in there. What I need to do is spend some time getting to know him and breaking down the wall that I'm assuming you or whoever else who counseled him has helped erect."

"You have a point," Reed responded.

"How about this? I spend a couple weeks with him, talk to him a little bit, get to know him. I'll send you a report every couple of days on his progress, as well as anything about his 'abilities.' Can we agree to that?" Ellis added.

"Somehow I'm getting the impression that I don't have a choice…"

"No, Reed, you don't. Talk to you in a couple days, brother," Ellis said as he turned to walk away and headed for the exit of the building.

Reed smirked, but it was an uncomfortable smirk. He knew the risk with having Ellis involved, but his hands were tied, and with the forces that he was dealing with wanting results, he had little choice in the matter. He knew this uncomfortable partnership with his old colleague would only lead to disaster. If not for Nahshon, then one of them.

CHAPTER 6

E llis's plan worked like a charm. For the following two weeks, he spent more time with Nahshon away from the facility and his group home. It provided an outlet for the young man to express himself, all the while giving Ellis more insight on the young man's true personality. Ellis was careful to not bring up any questions about his strange abilities. He felt like he had to establish a measure of trust with Nahshon and for the troubled youth to not see him as only a doctor or an authority figure.

Professional football season was underway, and Ellis had scored two tickets from a friend who was a season ticket holder. He noticed the young man's enthusiasm of the atmosphere and the various people out and about. It was the kind of energy that only sporting events can bring when you are actually there.

What really brought all the people in the place was the fact that it was the pro debut of the much talked about and newly acquired first round draft pick out of Clemson, Heisman Trophy winner Chace Galinsky. The phenom had had an out-of-this world season throughout his senior year and shattered previous NCAA records in the process. He was fast, quick, and had a shotgun for an arm. He was the total package, excelling in both running and throwing the ball. For one so young, it seemed unreal the poise and presence he showed on the field. A real field general in the making.

It was the first preseason game of the highly anticipated season with this young lion, and not only was the whole stadium watching, but the whole nation in general was tuned in to see the start of the rookie quarterback's career. Sports analysts were comparing him to names like Favre, Bradshaw, Williams, Brady, and Montana. And there Ellis and Nahshon were able to firsthand witness it themselves. They looked around the stadium and saw the various posters and pictures printed with the trending moniker, #CHACETHEDREAM, and marveled at how captivated the city had become with someone who hadn't even played yet.

"So what do you think? Is this your first time watching a football game live?" Ellis asked as he passed Nahshon the nachos and hot dog he bought for him.

"Incredible! I can't believe how wild these fans are about this guy. Is he really that good? I don't really follow pro football," Nahshon said as he scanned around the stadium at the rabid fans.

"Oh, he's the real deal. There were a lot of teams in the league interested in this guy. We just happened to suck so bad last season that we ended up with the number 1 draft pick this year."

Nahshon laughed at Ellis's comment. It was a reaction born out of, for once, being able to let his guard down, even if just for the span of a football game.

"Hey, take a look. They're about to kick off," Ellis said as he tapped Nahshon to get his attention.

And so the game began, and Galinsky did not disappoint. As if to send a message to the league of his coming, he unleashed a missile-like pass that nearly went for a touchdown on the opening play. The crowd was ecstatic, and the sound of the cheers was deafening. Ellis and Nahshon watched as the young quarterback put on a commanding performance throughout the first quarter, connecting a majority of times with his receivers while swiftly and elusively dodging tacklers with his innate swiftness as he evaded multiple attempts by the defense line. The overwhelmed defense was beginning to get frustrated, and it was obvious to the spectators just how good the young rookie was.

When the referee's whistle blew, the first quarter had wrapped up, and the score was 14 to 0. The roar of the crowd continued as Ellis and Nahshon sat back in their seats. They looked all around their row at the crazed fans. Even to the nonfootball fan, you could tell that this was a historic sports moment. Nahshon looked at the Jumbotron that showed as the young quarterback ran to the sidelines and was bombarded with adoring teammates. He took a big exhale and turned to Ellis.

"Whoa! This guy's phenomenal! And the energy in this place is crazy!" Nahshon yelled.

"I know! And I don't see it stopping. Now that he knows that he can run on them, he's most likely to pick this defense apart the rest of the game," replied Ellis.

Ellis's assessment was quite right. The young quarterback had figured out the weak link in the defense and was exploiting it with very fast and elusive running plays. The crowd was responding more to his skillful rushing as opposed to his long throws, and he fed off that. You could see on the opponents' sidelines the frustration that was mounting with the coach along with his players watching. They could not get this guy's number.

When one of the series fell short and the offense was on the sidelines on the other side, a couple of the defense guys got together among themselves and were discussing something as they looked across at Galinsky. As the second quarter was starting to wrap up, the referee signaled for Galinsky and his offense to return on the field. As they exited the huddle, the offense assembled on the line. Suddenly Nahshon's focus turned on to the view of the opposing football players on the line.

The first play was a play action pass which garnered a decent amount of yardage, something to throw off the defense that was expecting a run. Then on the next play, Galinsky ran an option play that allowed him to scramble with the ball for a first down. A smile of satisfaction was on Galinsky's face as he returned to the huddle. This worked the crowd into a frenzy. Ellis looked over and noticed Nahshon's stunned appearance. It was similar to that of his first meeting with him at Reed's interview room.

"He needs to stop running. He's got to go back to passing the ball," Nahshon said in a monotone almost under his breath.

"Nahshon, you okay?" Ellis said as he studied the boy's concerned demeanor.

The offense started the first down again with a running play as their running back forged on for another first down.

"Please," Nahshon said under his breath.

"Nahshon?" said a worried Ellis.

The offense returned back to the line, exuberant about their success and ready to continue another play.

"Don't," Nahshon said as his eyes locked directly on Galinsky's every move.

The offense went back to the huddle, ready to put the finishing touches on another score. They were closing in on the end zone, and their run offense was working flawlessly against the bewildered defense. There was supreme confidence on the young quarterback's face, as if everything were in the palm of his hands. Ellis looked at the frozen expression on Nahshon's face as he looked at Galinsky, and he turned his head to see what he was watching.

As the offense faced their opponents on the line, Galinsky ran through his cadence and with a loud yell, the play started, with Galinsky keeping the ball for another quarterback scramble.

"No," Nahshon whimpered.

As Chace Galinsky bobbed and weaved through the obstacles of teammates and opponents, two defenders quickly glanced at each other in signals to come up and try to make a pass at tackling him. They had something special in mind for the young upstart quarterback.

His stride was strong, and his breathing was steady, and there was a hole for him to shoot through as clear as day. Unbeknown to Galinsky, one of his linemen tripped backward, and the full weight of his body came crashing over his right foot, locking his movement in place. His motion came to an abrupt pause.

Instantly, two players on the defense, Tate Donaldson and Milo Galena, locked eyes on each other and signaled with a nod as they rushed in. Galena overtly tripped his own feet up, forcing himself to fall forward at the pileup of players. As he fell, he made sure his shoulder crashed into the side of Galinsky's pinned-down leg, forcing the rest of Galinsky's body in another direction.

The impact made a sickening sound as it caused his leg to snap like a twig in two places. The shriek that the young man made was horrific. A gasp was made in the stadium by all the spectators to what was taking place while the players that were engaging in the melee were still oblivious to what had just happened.

Galinsky leaned up in excruciating shock as Donaldson spear-headed right toward him. He had a clear shot at the young quarter-back and made no qualms about what had just happened to his leg. Donaldson braced himself as he prepared to ram into Galinsky.

"No!" yelled Nahshon, causing Ellis to turn his attention from the field back toward the young man.

Donaldson ran straight for the path of Galinsky's neck but oddly shifted to graze the outer rim of the helmet, popping the helmet off, causing the young quarterback's neck to turn to the side. The impact pushed Galinsky back down in the pile again as Donaldson rolled away. The crowd gasped again at the sight of the collision.

Players from both sides of the field ran out along with coaches and medical staff as both teams started confronting each other on the field with skirmishes. Some of the coaching staff tried to get control of players while medical personnel rushed to the pile of players to get to Galinsky. The broadcast stations quickly turned to commercial breaks to prevent showing much of the carnage. Referees were running all over the field, blasting their whistles while trying to restore order.

The stands were in utter chaos as spectators began screaming and yelling in the confusion of what had taken place down on the field. Ellis looked at Nahshon, who had a blank stare, almost as if in an exhausted catatonic state.

"Damn, dude!" said the spectator in the seat next to Nahshon as he stared at him.

A trail of blood was running down Nahshon's face from his nostril. Ellis quickly grabbed one of the napkins from his lap to catch the dripping blood and wipe Nahshon's face.

"Nahshon! Are you all right? What's wrong?"

"I'm okay. I don't know…," replied Nahshon.

"Let's go," Ellis said as he placed his concessions down in front of his seat and got up.

Ellis grabbed Nahshon by his shoulders and guided him past the irate onlookers in their row as he helped escort him to the exit of the stadium. There was little obstruction in their way as most of the people were too involved with the action happening on the field. They went through the exit gates and past security to get down to the street level outside the stadium.

A couple was walking along the sidewalk past Ellis and Nahshon and noticed the disheveled look on Nahshon's face.

"I'm sorry, is he all right?" asked the lady.

"Uh…yeah. My son sometimes gets real bad migraines at events like this," Ellis responded.

Nahshon lift his head up when he heard the doctor address him as "son." It was surprising to him but also reassuring.

"Oh! Those are the worst. She gets those all the time," replied the gentleman.

"Get better!" the couple yelled as continued away.

"Thank you," Nahshon said in a weakened tone as he rubbed his temple.

They made their way back to Ellis's car, and Ellis helped him along in the passenger seat. As he left the stadium parking lot, Ellis looked over at Nahshon with concern.

"Nahshon, how are you feeling now?"

"I'm feeling much better now. Are you going to take me back to the group home?" Nahshon asked.

"That's entirely up to you. We do have some time before I told the director I'd bring you back. Maybe we can go grab a bite to eat quick?" Ellis replied.

Nahshon thought about the generosity and concern that the doctor had shown him. It was a welcoming feeling that he'd rarely had in his life, a feeling that he wasn't sure he wanted to give up right away.

"Yeah, some food would be great right now," Nahshon said as he sat up more upright, appearing to feel much stronger.

The two drove to a family restaurant and had a seat. As they ordered their entrées and drinks from the waitress, there was an awkward silence between them. Neither was prepared to discuss what went on at the football game during the Galinsky incident.

As they sat there, people gathered around the bar area, which had a huge flat-screen TV. On the screen was a sports news channel that was discussing the incident at the game they had just left from.

One of the commentators, who had a reputation of being fiery and animated, was giving his take on the incident that occurred:

> *"And all y'all know that we all been through this in our playin' days, well...most of us on this panel do. No diss. But I gotta say this, and Johnny, our producer, get those sensors ready to bleep me out, but it's <BEEP! BEEP!> like that who made my career shorter than it coulda been. I can think of about seven players right off the back in my career that tried to take me out. And they all got away with it! The NFL got a send a message. Donaldson and Galena need to be kicked out of the league, PERIODT! I mean, we've been looking at this footage over and over again since it first happened. And I'm gonna ask the producers in the back one more time to play when Donaldson headhunted Galinsky. Y'all, show the footage."*

They cut to a slow-motion replay of the moment when Donaldson's helmet rammed into Galinsky's face. The direction that he was going somehow shifted slightly to the left, preventing the full brunt of force to impact under Galinsky's neck. When it first occurred from a distance in the crowd, it wasn't noticeable, but up close there was an eeriness to how the collision was averted.

> *"And all I'm sayin', and a lot of medical professionals are sayin', the direction he was going could've and should've severely injured that boy or*

possibly even killed 'em. Now this stuff pisses me the <BLEEP!> off! They need to be kicked out of the league today, as in RIGHT NOW!

"God was on the boy's side. That's the only way I can explain what happened to him. Now the leg— they were wrong for that to because they did head-hunted after his legs. The boy was on fire, running all over the place, and they knew they had to stop him. They were wrong for that! Speaking as some-one who got headhunted in my day, they need to go!

"Hunter, you can take it over from here, man. Got nothing else decent to say..."

Many of the patrons in the restaurant were left chuckling and laughing at the commentator's brash remarks, but Ellis sat there looking at the dread on Nahshon's face as he tried to stare downward, almost as if an expression of guilt.

"Nahshon, I can't skate around the issue any longer. Did you and the headaches have anything to do with what happened on that field today?" Ellis asked.

"I'm not sure. I don't know," Nahshon responded as his eyes began to tear.

Ellis looked sympathetically at the young man's desperate expression and graciously ceased the inquiry. The two went back to finishing their meal.

CHAPTER 7

He sat there in his parked car leaning his head back while trying to clear his head. Ellis turned his head aside to look out at the building he would be entering in a matter of minutes. It was the law office of his attorney, Wayne Atlas. Wayne Atlas was one of those lesser-known lawyers in the city whose legal commercials were splattered constantly on local TV during afternoons. Ellis thought that he would give contacting him a shot, and he figured that with this attorney, the strained back-and-forth with Dana would not last long. He did not want to go in the office before their scheduled time, who wants to go into a lawyer's office anyway, but this was a new day, and they'd agreed to discuss the disbursing of their late son's property. Even though it was a grim subject to discuss, Ellis was looking forward to the sight of his former wife, even if it was not going to be in a kind way.

The clock on his dashboard read 12:30. It was time to get the meeting started. Ellis got out of his car and ventured over to the front door the law office. As he entered, he noticed the lack of people in the place. There was only himself, Wayne Atlas sitting at his conference desk, and his receptionist across the room, typing away on her work desk.

Wayne Atlas was an interesting-looking character. He was starting to gain a reputation for his somewhat outlandish commercials, which usually showed someone in peril and Wayne dressed in an ancient Greek toga, tossing away the boulder on his back to come to the aid of the injured victim. The acting and costumes were so bad that it made the commercials a little comical to watch, but as he appeared that day, he wasn't dressed up as your average local attorney. He had on blue jeans, a leisure T-shirt, and a sports jacket that looked like he had just thrown it on right before Ellis came his office. There were legal documents and folders scattered all over the conference table, not fitting for someone who was supposed to have other people attend. In front of him was his laptop, which was open as if he was communicating with someone. Ellis took an available seat across from Atlas and sat down, trying to make sense of the questionable atmosphere.

"Wayne, where are Dana and her attorney at? Are they still supposed to be having this meeting with us?"

"Ellis, just so you know, I was contacted this morning by her attorney, Joeson O'Toole. The only way that she'll meet us in any discussion is by long distance. I was told that she has no desire to be in your presence and will only cooperate if the two of you can communicate through others far apart. I'm sorry to have to tell you that, man."

A well of sadness came over Ellis as once again he was reminded of the reality that had driven him and Dana apart. So much pain between the two of them over the loss of their son, but when they should be there for each other they were now at opposite ends—parents feuding over the last remnants of their dead ten-year-old child.

"I see she won't be coming into the office for this," Ellis said.

"Yeah, and she had explicit instructions that she not even see you in this deposition between both parties. So here's how were going to do this. You will sit next to me at a distance outside of the laptops view, so you can only be heard but not seen. I'll do most of the talking. I'm sure her attorney will be doing the same, and if things work out, we can have a clear split of your late son's items without the two of you needing to say a word," Atlas added.

"However you want to do this, I guess," said a dejected Ellis.

Just then the conference notification came on the computer, and Ellis took his place at his seat. As the screen came on, Ellis gazed at the image of Joeson O'Toole, and his suspicions were confirmed.

O'Toole was the son of Jamison O'Toole, a city councilman and a well-known public figure who had an infamous reputation for the derogatory rhetoric he was known for saying regarding racial issues within the city. The younger O'Toole reeked of privilege and possibly nepotism. His smug demeanor not only gave off the impression of a lawyer but someone who was accustomed to looking down on people. Ellis could tell from the start that the man would speak with forked tongue.

"Hello, Mr. Atlas, and I would assume the gentleman next to you is Mr. Daniels. I am Joeson O'Toole. Before we begin, there are some ground rules that we need to discuss. First, this will be a quick deposition regarding the disbursement of your late son's items among the two parties and strictly that. Other matters will be discussed later.

"Second, Ms. Geniro will not be seen on this communication. She has chosen to remain out of view as she has requested not to see or be seen by your client, Mr. Daniels. And third, your client is to not speak while I am speaking as I do not want to repeat myself. Is that something that your client can understand?"

Ellis reined in his anger as the young attorney spoke. He glanced over at Atlas for assistance in his compliance. His counsel nodded back for him to comply and remain calm. He looked back at the screen at the attorney and silently nodded in agreement.

"Good. Now that you understand, let's begin," the brazen attorney responded.

"This deposition is to finalize the disbursement of items belonging to Mr. Daniels and Ms. Geniro's deceased son, Grant. It has previously been agreed that Ms. Geniro will retain the entire collection of Grant's clothing attire. Toys and other objects of play will remain in the possession of Ms. Geniro as well. Grant's collection of comic books that his father, Mr. Daniels, and himself acquired will remain in the possession of Mr. Daniels as agreed. Which leads us to the remaining issue of the young boy's prized coin collection…"

Ellis's mind reeled back to the day that he'd given his son the coin book and his first set of minted coins. He remembered the look of wonder on Grant's face as he'd sat next to him on his bed and how the light reflected off the coins washed over his young face. He could feel the excitement as the boy studied the engravings on the surface of each coin.

Grant's hands coursed over the edges of the coin book as he studied the nooks inside the book for each coin to be placed in. Ellis knew it would be a prized possession to his son. He remembered holding the coin between his fingers and explaining the value to Grant and how to study its date by the year it was made and the attentive look on his son's face. It was one of the precious moments that they shared, moments he never shared with his own father. He and Grant shared a lifetime of moments together.

It was a sublime recollection, a cherished memory that brought his heart joy to revisit. Then his mind shifted to that fateful night and how he'd run through the crowd to find his boy lying lifeless on the ground. One of the bystanders was kneeling over him, trying to give him mouth-to-mouth resuscitation. He remembered pushing the person over so that he could try to revive the young boy himself. His compressions grew in vain as his son continued to not respond.

The carnival authorities had called the on-site paramedics, and they'd rushed in, pulling Ellis away so that they could try to save his son. He'd struggled with them because he did not want to stop touching his son, but they managed to pull him away for the professionals to save his son.

He remembered Dana screaming as she emerged from the sea of onlookers. When she ran up to him, she'd grabbed his shoulders and yelled, "What happened!" He'd looked down hopelessly at her and responded, "I don't know!" But he had known as he looked on the ground and his vaulted analytical mind began to work. He stood there in disbelief while one of the paramedics continued to block Dana from getting into contact with her son.

Ellis got up, ran to the screen, and yelled, "Why are you doing this? Dana, why are you doing this? He was my baby too! He was my baby too. I lost him too!"

His shoulders slumped in dejection while beside him, Atlas stood up and put his hand on his shoulder to both try to stop him and show support for his feelings while he ranted.

"Don't you think I've suffered? I loved those coins, and I loved how he loved those coins. Haven't we both suffered enough with this?" Ellis pleaded.

He could hear her sobbing on the other end of the screen. Joeson stood up, obscuring the image on the monitor, and furiously yelled back to the screen, "Atlas! Did I not tell your client to control himself? This is not what we agreed on. He was not to speak to my client directly. This will not do."

Joeson O'Toole backed away from in front of the screen almost if to show the view of him adjusting his expensive suit.

"We're going to have to continue this some other time when you have better control of your client. Goodbye," he said as he took a second to look at the screen in disdain.

"Wait! Stop!" Ellis yelled back. "Dana, don't do this. We don't need these people. We don't. Look at me. Look at me!"

Joeson reached over to the button on his computer and turned it off. And with that, the two on the other end of the conference were gone.

Ellis sat back in his seat, staring over at Atlas as he ventured back to his chair. There was a look of disappointment on Atlas's face, but he understood the raw emotions involved.

"Ellis, you know this was not going to continue like this. She's not ready to face you. The loss of your son is still fresh, my friend," Atlas remarked.

"I know," Ellis replied. He sat back in his chair and then he slumped over, putting his hands over his eyes.

"I just don't know when this will end. I miss my boy so much." It was said in a mournful tone.

Atlas excused himself to check his buzzing cell phone after it sounded a notification. Most likely it was a message from the other attorney with some not-so-kind words about Ellis's outburst. Ellis did not respond. Instead he sat there wallowing in thoughts about what never would be again…

CHAPTER 8

E llis stood there on the arched stone railings of the rotunda as he recounted the details of the failed deposition nearly a month ago to Nahshon as he sat on one of the rotunda steps. It was important for Ellis to establish a connection of openness between himself and Nahshon so that the young man could see that he was giving as much of himself as he was expecting.

"So all that happened because of some coins?" Nahshon asked in bewilderment.

"Yeah. All because of this," Ellis responded as he held up one of his late son Grant's prize minted coins.

"It sounds to me like it was something deeper than your ex-wife only wanting the coins," added Nahshon.

Ellis was impressed with the young man's intuitive rationale. He could see that their continued time together was forging a closer connection between the two of them. He knew that eventually he would have to give some kind of report to Reed. The voice messages that Reed had left for him sounded almost agitated, as if he was growing tired of the lack of information. Despite the terms of their agreement for his help, he realized that Nahshon was still Reed's case.

He juggled the coin between his fingers as he thought about the now infamous near-fatal collision on the football field that cut short the career of rookie sensation Chace Galinsky. He then stopped with the juggling as his eyes left the coin and veered toward Nahshon as he was looking at his phone.

"Nahshon, what is it that you see when you look out into the world?"

"The same as you, I guess. It's just sometimes I happen to see numbers. A lot of numbers," Nahshon replied.

"Where, Nahshon?"

"Everywhere. Sometimes I have to concentrate to make the numbers fade away," Nahshon added.

"These numbers stay in the same place? Are they easy to read and remember?"

"No. They are always changing constantly. Either up and or down, constantly shifting," said Nahshon.

"How long have you had this perception Nahshon?"

"I don't know. I guess since the first foster home they sent me to in the first grade," Nahshon replied.

This intriguing revelation piqued Ellis's interest. His analytical mind started to fire off and theorize, and hypotheses started rolling in the recesses of his mind. But before he could conclude anything, there was some confirmation that he needed to gather. He took the coin from his hand and stood up along the granite of the rotunda they were sitting on.

"Nahshon, I'm going to spin this coin, and whatever I ask you, I want you to answer with complete honesty. Can you do that for me?" Ellis asked.

"Yeah. Sure," Nahshon responded, slightly confused.

Without Nahshon getting comfortable in his reply, Ellis spun the coin and looked at the young man.

"See anything?"

"No. Nothing at all except a spinning coin," responded Nahshon.

Ellis picked back up the coin and gave it another spin. This time he added more force to the spin so that the coin would remain spinning longer.

"Here's the thing I like about this coin. It's a lot like fate. You really can't tell which way it's going to go until it gets there...much like fate. Because, after all, we all know no one can control fate, right? By the way, what do you see now?" he quickly asked Nahshon.

"Noth—wait! I do see numbers around it! They're sort of faint, but I see them around the coin as it's spinning—35, 72, 15, 48, 68, 91. The numbers keep changing," Nahshon said, excited.

"What *color* were they? Ellis asked as the coin fell flat.

"I don't know…darkish gray, maybe? Nothing really spectacular."

"Apparently not to you," Ellis responded as he spun the coin again. "But here's what I really want to know: what's your favorite? Heads or tails?"

"Heads definitely. I've always preferred heads," Nahshon said as his gaze returned to the spinning coin. "Wait! I do see something different. The numbers are changing color. There were a few numbers that were reddish, but now the numbers around the coin are green!" Nahshon said, shocked as the coin once again return to its side.

The coin was on its heads side, which was encouraging for Nahshon to see. Ellis's expression was blank as he took in the new data he was gathering from both the coin and Nahshon's reaction.

"Wow. You called it. It indeed was heads, your favorite," Ellis said as he retrieved the coin to continue with a mighty forceful spin.

"Here's the thing: *I hate tails. Tails terrify me. Tails are dangerous. Tails are threatening. Tails can be fatal! In fact, my very life is in danger if this coin lands on tails!*" Ellis yelled in a threatened and excited voice.

Nahshon was shocked by Ellis's outburst as his attention shifted to the spinning coin. Numbers increased around the coin while the coloration teetered to a more reddish hue as the spinning slowed down. This made Nahshon more anxious as his stare fixated on the numbers while more of the tails side was visible.

Suddenly Ellis noticed almost an unexplained shift in the spin of the coin as if it was changing its trajectory from one end to the other. He looked over at Nahshon and noticed the intense stare the young man had on the coin as if he had complete focus on it spin. Eerily the coin's spin ended with it on its heads side. Both of them stared at the coin in slight astonishment.

"Nahshon. Real important question here. What did you see?"

"I saw lots of red numbers around the coin along the tails side, but then the numbers changed to green and then the coin landed on its heads side," Nahshon said in a stunned voice.

"Why?"

"Because I wanted it to," answered Nahshon in a low worried tone. Nahshon looked up at Ellis almost as if lost in that moment. When he locked eyes with Ellis, Ellis could see that some blood was gathered around one of his nostrils as if preparing to run down his face. Ellis handed him a napkin from his back pocket as he quickly retrieved the coin and placed it back in his front pocket.

"I think that's enough for today," Ellis said as he gave a comforting smile to Nahshon.

"What do you think is going on?" asked Nahshon.

"Not sure, Nahshon. But we'll figure it out, I promise."

Later that evening, Ellis returned to his office to file some case documents. As he approached the door to his office, he saw Reed coming from the other end with a questionable expression on his face. In his hand were some notes he took from his earlier encounter with Nahshon and his thoughts on what had taken place with the spinning coin. As he got closer to his office door and Reed, his grasp on his files tightened as if to protect them.

"There you are. I thought I was gonna have to turn around and head back home."

"Not at all. I had a few office things that needed my attention," Ellis responded.

"Yeah. I had to do the same thing myself earlier."

There was uncomfortable pause between the two as if they were taking a moment to read each other. Ellis noticed Reed's eyes shift between his eyes and the file that he clutched in his hand.

"Our boy, Nahshon. You've been spending a lot of clinical time with him."

"Not all clinical time," Ellis interjected.

"Right. Was he out with you earlier today by any chance?"

Ellis knew that Reed had the answer to that question and that it would be fruitless to deceive him. It almost came across as if he were expecting a lie to emerge.

"As a matter of fact, he was. It's all a part of my plan to create more of a rapport with him and get him to open himself up more.

Let me remind you, Reed, we agreed to my discretion on how my methods are used with this client," Ellis said in a direct tone.

"Oh no, I'm not trying to step on that, Ellis. That's why I asked for your help because you do get results. It's just that I got to remind you that he is registered as one of my cases, and as such, I am responsible with his group home or any records of him being out of their building for any extended length of time," Reed explained.

"Understood. Sorry, I should have notified you beforehand."

"Liability issues really. Is that file you're holding about Nahshon?" Reed asked as his gaze fixed on the file in Ellis's hand.

"Yes. Jumbled thoughts really. A few things I jotted down. I'll probably spend a while gathering them up and making it into more of a cohesive file report," Ellis replied. By now he knew that Reed was reading his reactions for hints that he would be trying to lie to him.

"No worries, but I would like a copy of that report for myself. Something to give to the bigwigs on Nahshon's progress."

Reed placed his hand on Ellis's shoulder and then started to walk away. He suddenly turned back around as if he remembered something.

"I just remembered one of the things I meant to ask you. I know it's been a few weeks since we chatted, but I had to get your take on the injury Galinsky suffered in that game last month."

"Gruesome. And tragic," Ellis responded.

"That's an understatement. They are saying his future in pro football's over. That leg will never be the same. His agent is trying to broker some kind a of commentary gig for him, but with his lack of experience and coming in the league as a rookie, it's looking unlikely."

"Like I said, tragic," Ellis responded.

"Well, what everyone's talking about is how it could've been a whole lot worse. Somehow the head shot missed. A lot of experts are saying that would've been fatal. Say, didn't you and Nahshon go to the game? You guys were there. How bad was it?"

"Not for the faint of heart, Reed."

"True. But living is better," Reed replied as he put his hands in his pocket. "Lucky kid. What are the chances of that, huh? Anyway, we should hang out more, outside of the business. Later," Reed said as he confidently continued walking down the hallway.

Ellis remembered that Reed was no fool. He had done a good job of reading him. Not only that, it confirmed his fear that Reed knew Nahshon had something to do with the Galinsky accident. He knew that he would have to give him a report, but how much of it would have to be considered.

But Reed had made an error in letting him become aware that Nahshon's case wasn't just for Reed's selfish agenda but that there were other forces at play. He contemplated his new dilemma as he turned the knob of his office door to get to work.

CHAPTER 9

The hours into the night were getting long, and the yawns were getting more frequent as Ellis probed deep within his stack of rented books. It was a common practice back in his college days, and the method felt like a familiar friend.

There was something that Reed said that Ellis could not shake. He played over their encounter in the hallway over and over again in his mind as he tried to formulate how much his own colleague knew. He wiped a tear from his eye as he yawned while fatigue started to kick in. He leaned back in his chair and looked up at the ceiling as he focused on one word Reed ended their conversation with.

"He said *chance*. Something about that word. Chance... Chance...something about that word," Ellis said to himself as he rummaged through pages of one of the books in front of him.

Probability allows us to quantify the likelihood an event will occur. You might be familiar with words we use to talk about probability, such as "certain," "likely," "unlikely," "impossible," and so on. You probably also know that the probability of an event happening spans from impossible, which means that this event will not happen under any circumstance, to certainty, which means that an event will happen without a doubt.

The probability of a certain event occurring depends on how many possible outcomes the event has. If an event has only one possible outcome, the probability for this outcome is always 1 (or 100 percent). If there is more than one possible outcome, however, this changes.

Probability can also be written as a percentage, which is a number from 0 to 100 percent. The higher the probability number or percentage of an event, the more likely is it that the event will occur."

One common theory is the interpretation of probabilities as relative frequencies, for which one could then suggest the manipulation of such frequencies.

"The interpretation and manipulation of probabilities as frequencies," Ellis said to himself as he processed the information he just read.

He got up out of his seat and paced the floor, slowly flicking his pencil between his fingers back and forth as he figured out the significance of the theories compared to what he witnessed from Nahshon.

Over and over he tapped the pencil against his thigh as he whispered the words *interpretation* and *manipulation* repeatedly until an epiphany came along that stopped his movement around his living room. He returned to his seat and moved over some of the previous books he had gone through to find what he was looking for.

Underneath the books were papers containing case studies of people who either claimed to possess psychic abilities or documented examples that were not generally accepted by the scientific community as factual. Most of these claims were deemed too radical or irrational and could not be taken seriously by medical science means.

There were various reported claims of people who displayed phenomenon such as telepathy, pyrokinesis, telekinesis, examples of psychic surgery from the Middle East, levitation, Chinese energy medicine involving the use of chi, reports of divination in the form of religious practice in southern holiness churches, astral projection, mediumship, as well as claims of psychometry. Despite this, there wasn't anything connecting what Ellis noticed in Nahshon's case.

That moment was eluding Ellis, that moment when synapses start firing and analyzing begins. It usually took a stray thought to connect another stray thought and another and another until his reasoning kicked in.

Then the solution hit him: He already had everything he needed, and it was with him when he first met Nahshon. Next to some of his books was a CD case containing the interview he walked in on with Reed and Nahshon. It wasn't necessary to listen to the whole interview again, but there was something on that Ellis needed to explore again.

He pressed Forward and Play as he listened to different benchmarks in the interview until he was able to cue up the part that he needed to hear...

> *"The images, do you see them around you now, Nahshon, and are the values shifting right now?"*
>
> *"Constantly."*
>
> *"So is it something that you can't necessarily control, right? Then how are you able to understand them?"*
>
> *"At first I didn't, but as I got older, I started to recognize things happen because of what I saw."*
>
> *"I think it's a good thing that we keep this between us. The medical community. The science community. I don't think they could comprehend this phenomenon that you have. Is okay to call it that?"*
>
> *"There's nothing 'phenomenal' about it, Dr. Richardson. It's draining."*
>
> *"Draining?"*
>
> *"Do you even understand what I'm saying right now? I don't think you understand how life works."*

52

> *"Young man, I—"*
>
> *"No, you don't. Everything is chaos. Millions and millions of possibilities waiting to happen at any given moment."*
>
> *"I'm sorry, but I simply don't believe that. There are calculated results to a plan. Science dictates that."*
>
> *"Science also dictates that every action carries a reaction, so why is it so hard to believe that every movement creates a series of different possible results?"*

Nahshon's retort made Ellis smirk to himself, the same as it did when he originally heard it.

> *"So…you can't control your ability?"*
>
> *"I told you before I can't control it."*
>
> *"Have you ever really tried to challenge your limits? Explore your potential?" Reed urged.*
>
> *"I'm telling you it happens all the time. Why are you pushing me so much! You're no different than the rest of them, especially the ones that tried to use me!"*

"Nahshon is playing me," Ellis muttered to himself.

Obviously Nahshon had been aware of his abilities for quite some time but was very guarded on how much Ellis should be made aware. More revelations revealed themselves to Ellis:

- One thing that was apparent was that Reed was and is trying to exploit those abilities for his own purposes.
- Judging from the young man's temperance, Reed was just one of the many who either have or were currently trying to exploit him.
- Nahshon is fearful of what he can potentially do.

After contemplating his analysis, Ellis came to the conclusion that if he was going to get to the root of Nahshon's business, the kid gloves were going to have to come off and their next encounter would not be as passive as the last few times.

Besides, no one played Ellis Daniels twice.

CHAPTER 10

The alarm clock went off around 5:00 a.m., bringing with it a pleasant melody, a stark contrast to the boisterously loud alarm clock that she shared in her bedroom with Ellis. Dana sat up in her bed and looked across the room to her window at the outside world and wondered what was out there waiting for her.

She stood up and ventured forward to the window where her desk sat propped in front. As she sat in the rolling chair in front of the desk, Dana flipped open her laptop to see her planned events of the day.

She looked back up again at the window and looked around once again at the outside world on the other side. Reassured, she made an expression of resolve to get started.

"Okay," she said.

By 6:00 a.m., she was out of the house and going on her daily jog in the morning around her neighborhood. The air was brisk as she donned a skullcap, which she figured she could remove and place in the pocket of her jacket once her body temperature rose from the jogging.

She used to only cover a three-block radius from her house, but she had begun to challenge herself, so she opted to cover four blocks instead. There were other joggers along the trail, and by now she had begun to know some of them personally by name.

One new addition that came with her four-block run was the bodega nestled along the outskirts of her neighborhood. She rewarded herself for the added distance in her jog with a warm cup of caramel mocha that she would sip on her way back to her house. The owner of the bodega was a slightly younger man, fairly attractive, who had taken to making eyes at her. Though it was nice to receive the attention, she knew that she was not yet ready to date again.

The time was now 8:00 a.m., and after a shower and change of clothes, Dana was at the workout session that she attended three days a week. Her small band of workout buddies consisted of a colleagues from her office and two other professionals whose schedule also allowed them a quick workout before heading to their offices.

Dana made it through the doors of her medical office around 10:00 a.m., and waiting for her patiently were members of her staff. Originally when she first began her stint at the office four years ago, they were often loud around the office, even annoying sometimes, but in recent times have become very quiet and reserved, especially when she showed up, as if they were too nervous to be their natural selves around her.

When she approached their station, one of them handed her a folder with the order of appointments that she had for the day. They stood there quietly as she scrolled through the list of appointments, almost as if they were on eggshells.

"Good morning, ladies," Dana said.

"Good morning, Doctor," the four ladies almost said in unison.

"And how was the weekend for you ladies?"

"Good, Doctor," replied the four ladies almost in unison again.

"Holly went out on her third date," said one of the staff as she looked at the coworker she was talking about.

"Same guy? The band drummer?" Dana asked.

"Yes, ma'am," Holly replied.

"No nooky, right?" Dana asked as her eyes peeked upward from the files she was reading as she spoke.

"Oh no, ma'am."

"But you wanted to?"

"Oh hell yes!" Holly replied in wild excitement.

Dana and all the ladies around her erupted into laughter as the staff returned to the jovial mood that they were used to working around. Dana high-fived Holly and clutched her files as she turned to walk away.

"I will be in my office if you need me, ladies," said Dana.

"Yes, ma'am," they all replied in unison.

"Oh! Dr. Ginero, you have a 12:30 appointment with Kelsey. I wasn't sure if you needed to reschedule her for another date," said Roslyn, another one of the ladies on staff.

"Why would you do that? Of course I'll see Kelsey! She's one of my favorite patients. Keep the appointment on the books. I can't wait to see her!" Dana said as she continued down the hallway.

"Of course, Doctor," Roslyn replied.

As Dana went into her office, the ladies gathered around each other to gossip.

"Poor dear," said Roslyn. "I don't know if I could go on if I lost one of my babies."

"I couldn't."

"Me either!"

"Shhh! Y'all too loud. Don't you know how thin these walls are? We better get back to work."

The ladies scattered and went back to the duties that they were performing before Dana's arrival.

Kelsey was a twenty-one-year-old single mother whose boy-friend had deserted her once he got news of her pregnancy. Both her parents were deceased, and she had worn out her welcome at her sister's house. One of her girlfriends offered her a place to stay for the time being.

She'd been diagnosed with serious thyroid problems which made the pregnancy difficult and dangerous for the baby, but despite all these obstacles, she'd maintained a perseverance that Dana had come to admire and was inspired by.

Some of their appointments ended up with a heart-to-heart talk and advice given by Dana, and were it not for the fact that there were other patients scheduled following Kelsey, Dana would spend all day chatting with the young mother.

The last appointment that they had, Dana could tell she was more nervous than usual. The idea of complications with the baby was starting to get the better of Kelsey, but Dana reassured her everything would work out fine. The last time they monitored the baby, it was in a questionable position, and there was fear that her hyperthyroidism could cause fetal abnormalities or congestive heart failure in her unborn child.

After a brief pep talk, they began the ultrasound as she ran along the surface of the young mother's belly. The position that the baby was in would dictate whether or not surgical options would have to be taken. Any more stress to the baby was something that Dana did not want to happen.

She was looking closely for the baby's head and shoulder placement, and when she saw that they was in perfect alignment she breathed a sigh of relief and smiled at Kelsey. She breathed a sigh of relief and smiled at Kelsey.

"In the perfect position. Everything is going to be fine," she said to the nervous mother.

She smiled back at Dana because she knew how emotionally invested her doctor had become. She reached her arms out, and Dana welcomed her with an embrace. The strong young mother broke down in her arms and sobbed continuously. Dana stroked the back of her head and reassured her.

"You are going to be such a good mother. I promise," Dana replied in a comforting tone.

After the medical office closed, Dana drove home and, on the way, stopped by the bodega that she went to earlier that day by foot when she was jogging. She purchased a bottle of wine and some gourmet bread, and after she had made her purchase and got her receipt, she saw a phone number written on the back. It was from the owner who was attracted to her.

And as she briefly contemplated giving him a call, she overheard two teenagers talking about the latest video of Uncle Dan destroying a racist white supremacist on TV. Immediately she knew who they were referring to, and it snapped her back to reality. She took her groceries and sternly left.

Once Dana got home that evening, she put the bottle wine in the freezer and went upstairs to take a hot shower. Emerging from the shower clean and relaxed, she next put on her nightgown and went back downstairs to pour herself a glass of wine. She got some gourmet cheese out of the refrigerator and placed it on a small plate.

Next, she cut herself a slice of gourmet bread and placed it on the same plate with the cheese. She went to her stereo and selected a playlist of contemporary jazz to relax the atmosphere. Lastly, she poured herself a glass of wine and stood, still preparing herself to sit down and unwind.

As she lifted her glass to take a sip, she was bombarded with thoughts of her deceased son, her child that she will never see again. Dana violently threw the glass down at the wall, collapsed on the floor, crawled herself into a ball, and sobbed mournfully into the night.

CHAPTER 11

"This is an interesting part of the park you insisted on us to meet. I thought we were going to be at the spot where you did the coin test?" asked Nahshon.

"Nope. I thought a little change of scenery would do us some good since this part of the park is known for people taking rides through."

"If you say so," Nahshon replied.

"After all, I felt this would be appropriate, since you've been taking me for a ride," Ellis said with a hint of condemnation.

"I don't know what you're talking about Ellis," Nahshon said in a defensive tone.

"No?" replied Ellis as he took out his pocket tape recorder and pressed Play:

> "Everything is chaos. Millions and millions of possibilities waiting to happen at any given moment."
>
> "I'm sorry, but I simply don't believe that. There are calculated results to a plan. Science dictates that."
>
> "Science also dictates that every action carries a reaction, so why is it so hard to believe that every movement creates a series of different possible results?"

Nahshon slumped back into the park bench with a withdrawn expression on his face. It was similar to his reaction when Ellis first watched him in Reed's office.

"I didn't know you was in on that conversation…"

"Yeah, I did overhear it, and actually I forgot about it. While I was doing some research, it came back to me, some of the things that were said between you two. What I want to know is why, Nahshon, did you feel like you have to deceive me? I'm only here to help you."

"Yeah right. 'Help me'? You mean 'use me,'" said Nahshon.

"'Use you'? No, Nahshon!" Ellis vehemently denied.

"No? That's what everybody has done ever since I was a little boy being tossed around in the system from this foster home to that foster home. Most of them didn't know what was going on, but some had a feeling something wasn't right with me. The ones who became aware of the things I saw thought that they could use me to bring them luck or help them win the lottery or fortune-telling or something crazy which I don't even think I can do.

"When they realized that I couldn't give them what they wanted, I was expelled from their houses and put back into the foster care system. This happened with four different families. And then they assigned me this Dr. Richardson guy, who at first seemed like someone I could trust and seemed to care about me.

"More and more he began questioning my abilities and what I could do in his experiments. It felt like the things my foster parents wanted me to do. 'This winning lottery number,' 'figure out this,' 'what direction should I take,' 'what team is gonna win?'—all the while pushing me and pushing me and not giving a damn about my feelings or what I wanted and needed. Like some kind of a damn prop!

"And so I shut down, and I wouldn't give him what he wanted, and what does he do? He passes me off to his smarter 'colleague' with some hopes of getting me to control my power abilities so that he could use them again himself. Just another user," the young man said with desperation and hopelessness in his cracked voice.

Ellis could see the pain in the boy's face, and it made him realize how much emotional pain he was in. Being in the dark was not that big a deal compared to the dysfunction and anguish that Nahshon had been through.

"Nahshon, I'm so sorry about what you been through. I'm not a user. I generally care about you, almost like a son. And that's unfair to you, because no one should be trying to play a father figure to you. I can tell you've had enough of that in your life. You have an amazing gift. Where it comes from, what all you can do, I do not know, and it sounds like to me you don't know either, and that's frightening.

"This is a world of users, of people like Reed Richardson, but I'm not one of them. I want to help you, Nahshon. Help you master whatever it is that you've been gifted with so that not only can you control it, but you can have a normal life despite having it. But that requires trust," Ellis said as he looked directly at Nahshon.

"You trusting me and me trusting you," said Ellis as he noticed the young man's posture on the park bench get more relaxed.

Ellis sat himself back in the park bench and took a deep breath, and as he exhaled, he looked out at the overlook of the park and with his head, leaned up toward the sky.

"I'll tell you about the night my son died, Nahshon…Grant, G-Man we called him, loved the state fair. It had become a tradition in our family. We found that he got more excited going there in the evenings than during the daytime, especially with everything being lit up.

"One thing he really look forward to was us buying him an Italian sausage in a bun. It was something that he knew was my favorite, and he immediately latched on to it. It was a guilty pleasure we enjoyed eating together, and I think it was his way of being more like dad.

"There was talk earlier that day of some of the rides and attractions being shut down due to a heavy rainstorm earlier that morning, but the park board did a decent job of covering everything from the downpour, and all the attractions would still remain open.

"Dana wasn't interested at all in Italian sausages. Rather, she had a thing for funnel cakes, and the evening would not be complete unless she had one, so we decided to briefly separate. While she got in line for her funnel cake, me and G-man would get in line for our sausages.

"Both booths were located a distance from each other, so G-man had to cover some distance from the booth where Dana was in line. There were all kind of smells in the air from multiple food booths, but none of them were catching our attention. We knew what the smell of the Italian sausage on the grill was like, and it hadn't reached our noses yet.

"Suddenly G-man yelled, 'Dad! That's it!' when he looked beyond the crowd and saw the Italian sausage stand lit up in marquee lights. I closed my eyes and took a whiff, and sure enough the smell of the sausage was in the air. As I opened my eyes back up, G-man got excited and took off running toward the stand ahead of me.

"The crowd was not as dense as the last couple of years, probably because of the rain, so I could see a good view of G-man running toward the Italian sausage stand. As I stood there watching G-man sprint, I chuckled to myself and peeked the other way toward the direction of the funnel cake stand that Dana was at.

"The split second I turned my head back to look for G-Man, he was gone... The cable providing power to all the booths in that sector of the fair was normally covered with mats so people did not trip over it, but that night, because of the wet conditions and the influx of people, the mat had shifted and left part of the power cable exposed.

"When Grant was running, somehow he tripped in front of the exposed cable. Near the exposed area where the mat had shifted, there was a small puddle left over from the earlier rain close to the water. When my son tripped over and fell into the cable, it touched the puddle of water, sending currents through the water as well as G-man.

"I burst through the crowd to find my son electrocuted and not breathing. I ran as fast as I could to find someone trying to resuscitate him. I pushed the man aside and tried to administer CPR myself to G-man, but he never responded. I heard a shriek that I recognized and looked up, and it was Dana. Just like me, she had come through the crowd to find our child lying lifeless.

"She yelled at me to tell her what happened, but I had no answer. She screamed at me to do something, but I couldn't. Someone grabbed me from behind and pulled me away. It was two of the paramedics on site. Other paramedics rushed to attend to G-man. I stood back up and went to hold Dana as we watched helplessly while they tried to revive our son.

"They put G-man on a stretcher and boarded him into the ambulance as park security cleared the crowds for them to make a hasty exit to the hospital. There was only room in the back of the ambulance for one of us to sit with the paramedics, so of course Dana rode with them while I was in the front seat with the ambulance driver.

"We had only made it to blocks away from the fair when I heard Dana in the back of the ambulance screaming and wailing hysterically. I looked at the ambulance driver, and the expression on his face, it looked like an expression that he had often shown in his line of work. I sank my head into the palm of my hands the rest of the way there because I knew my son was gone.

"When we arrived at the hospital, I got out the passenger seat and rushed to the back of the ambulance, where some hospital personnel were already waiting. As the doors opened up, the paramedics brought down the stretcher with G-man on it with a blanket over his head.

"One of the paramedics came out with Dana, who was in a state of nonverbal shock. The paramedic brought Dana over to me, and I held her as they officially recorded the time of death for Grant and wheeled the stretcher with his body into the hospital building past us…"

Ellis could've added more to the story, but he just couldn't do it. He could've gone on about the resentment that Dana harbored toward him as she blamed him from allowing Grant to slip away from him. How it tore two families apart, the bickering and finger-pointing that continued to this day. And how without the joy that their son brought to the family, the two could no longer coexist in their home, causing the marriage to wither away and eventually end in divorce.

But he couldn't. The wound was still too fresh.

Nahshon placed his hand on Ellis's shoulder. He could tell how taxing it was for Ellis to recollect that painful experience.

"Ellis, I'm sorry that you had to relive that again. I trust you now. You gotta understand, everyone who's either become aware or I've shared this ability with has used it for their own gain, and the truth is, I don't even have it figured out.

"I don't know if I had anything to do with what happened at the game. All I know is that I saw the guy heading toward Galinsky, and I did not want that to happen. This sight that I have…scares me, and I'm tired of being scared of it. I'm ready to learn to control it."

Ellis returned the gesture and placed his hand on Nahshon's shoulder.

"Then let me be clear, Nahshon. I don't want to hurt you. I'm not trying to exploit you, and I'm not trying to use your abilities for my gain. You have an amazing gift, and you've paid a tremendous price for that gift. I want to help you master that gift so that it doesn't have to be a curse on your life. If you let me allow me to help, I promise to help you figure out how you got this, why you got this, and what you can do with it to help not only yourself but the world. You may be able to visualize chances, but I'll always believe that everything happens for a reason," Ellis said as he extended his hand for a handshake.

Nahshon both appreciated and believed in the pledge that Ellis had just made. He responded by answering his gesture with a handshake.

"Where do we begin?" Nahshon asked.

"We can begin here," answered Ellis. "Look around us, we're in an area full of possibilities."

Nahshon lifted his head to turn his gaze around at the overlook area of the park that they were meeting at. The park was lively with people all around enjoying the pleasant autumn day. Some people were strolling while children were in the playground area swinging and climbing the jungle gyms. There were some couples sitting on park benches, enjoying the romantic scenery of the overlook of the city.

Nahshon's attention shifted to a dog chasing its owners as they ran along laughing. As they ran along the dog park area, they parted ways to throw off the pursuing canine. Ellis watched Nahshon's attention at the dog's owners and what they were doing.

"Quick, Nahshon, which way is the dog going?" Ellis yelled.

Nahshon's eyes focused on the area around the dog as numbers appeared around its aura. In seconds, the focus the numbers on one side turned red as its counterpart numbers became greenish.

"With the lady on the left," he replied.

And sure enough, the dog's attention went with the female owner as it veered toward the left and caught up with her. She kneeled down to accept the canine's approach and patted its back to the dog's delight. The man she was with who ran in the other direction started to walk back toward them with a disappointed look on his face.

"See? I told you he liked you better than me. Stupid mutt," he said sarcastically as he kneeled down to pet his dog as well.

Nahshon seemed pleased by the success of his prediction and the owners' adoration for their dog. He looked up at Ellis, who nodded and looked further toward the children's playground area.

"The children playing on the swing. Tell me something unusual that's about the happen."

Nahshon fixed his gaze at the group of children on the swings, particularly the middle swing. A young girl was swinging along as a little boy in front of her caught and pushed her back to help her gain momentum. Numbers began to form around a little boy and behind the girl as she swung. Both sets of varying numbers began to turn reddish. Nothing seemed out of the ordinary as the little boy continued to help her get higher and higher on her swings.

"See the little girl in the middle?" Nahshon replied. "Something bad is going to happen in front and behind her."

"Are the sets of numbers reddish in color?" Ellis asked.

"Yeah. But it is a faint red, and it doesn't feel like something that dangerous."

Ellis looked on along with Nahshon. Running toward the swings was a group of young boys, one of which was the little girl's brother. They ran through the swing area, with the brother running toward the rear as his friends ran in the front. As the little girl's swing started to go back, her brother jumped to catch it as it lifted up in the air and added his momentum to push it down even faster.

"Jason! What are you doing? Stop, I'm telling Mom!" yelled the little girl.

As the little girl's speed increased coming downward, her friend in front shifted his sights to the little boys that ran past him, drawing his attention away from the little girl returning toward him. The little girl's feet came crashing into the boy's back and shoulders, sending him flying forward to the ground.

The boy's fall forward made a large thump. He quickly recovered, sitting himself up while rubbing his knees that were scraped from the ground. Children around began to laugh at the spectacle they had just seen. The collision was not enough to hurt him other than a few scrapes and his pride. The little girl's momentum nearly stopped as she jumped off to attend her playmate.

"Quincy, are you okay?" the concerned little girl asked her friend.

"I hate your brother!" The little boy sniffled as he watched the girl's brother and his friends run away. As he got up and rubbed his aching knees, he noticed a rock on the ground and picked it up while giving chase to his assailants. By then the numbers around the children had dissipated.

"There was incredible, Nahshon. You focused on a segment of people and predicted an occurrence happening accurately. That was awesome," Ellis said.

"Yeah, but we better do the responsible thing and stop those kids from having a big fight," Nahshon said as he watched the little boy preparing to throw the rock as he closed in on the group of boys that caused his accident.

"Perhaps you're right. Let's go," Ellis replied as they got up from their bench to go squash the fight among the kids.

Later Ellis and Nahshon continued walking around the park. Ellis stopped walking and grabbed Nahshon's shoulders to slow his pace.

"Now let's try something a lot harder. Do you feel the wind? How heavy it is? Which way is it blowing?"

"In our direction. I can feel it blowing in my face," Nahshon replied.

"Good. See that couple there on the bench? The lady with a hat, which way would you say the wind is blowing at her?"

Nahshon looked at the older couple sitting on the bench. The lady had a summer hat with its tip blowing backward from her brow.

"The wind is blowing in her face. She's in the same direction as we are. You can tell by it blowing her hat backward," Nahshon replied.

"Right. I want to see you try to make her hat fly off in the opposite direction of the wind."

"What? That's impossible!" scoffed Nahshon.

"Not for you. I believe in you Nahshon. Try it," said Ellis.

Nahshon drew a deep breath as his eyes focused on the older woman sitting on the bench. The focus caused a tunnel affect, and everything around her was blurred, including her companion alongside her. As his focus increased, a variety of numbers appeared around her constantly changing their numeric value. As his focus intensified, some of the numbers behind her started to take on a greenish hue as their numeric value began increasing.

Nahshon began to notice greenish numbers appearing in the air behind the lady, almost as if they were waiting for something to appear. His eyes shifted to the changing numbers in the air. Ellis could only stand back and watch as Nahshon appeared to be staring off into thin air around the lady.

Two men close by were tossing a Frisbee at each other not too far from where the old couple were sitting. As one of the men released the Frisbee from his hand, the numbers in Nahshon's perception turned dark green and varied in the 80s and 90s. Just then a gust of wind knocked the hat backward.

Before the hat could fly behind her, the Frisbee that was thrown veered more to the side and nicked the hat in the air around the spot that Nahshon was focusing on. The contact of the Frisbee knocked the hat forward and sideways as it went against the current of the wind and fell forward down toward the base of the overlook. It tipped off the base of the overlook and fell off the cliff.

It all happened in one motion, leaving Ellis and Nahshon dumbfounded. The couple got up and rushed to look where the hat had flown over the cliff of the overlook. They watched as it was no longer in the path of the wind and continued to fall all the way down into the wooded area below.

The two men tossing the Frisbee rushed to get it back. They looked confused as to how it went so far out of its trajectory. As the couple watched the hat fall farther, they stopped and looked at each other.

"See? That's why you shouldn'ta went out with that hat today. I knew you was going to lose it!" said the old man from the bench.

"Oh, shut up, Al!" said the disgusted old woman.

The couple continued arguing between themselves as Ellis and Nahshon took in what just occurred. Ellis reached into his pocket and pulled out his wallet. He went in and pulled out a $50 bill. He walked over to the old couple and extended his hand with the bill.

"I just saw what happened, and I feel so terrible about it. Please take this donation and get yourself a new hat if you can."

"Oh, that's sweet of you, dear, but we can't accept that from you," said the old woman.

"The hell we can't!" The old man said as he snatched $50 bill out of Ellis's hand.

"C'mon, girl, we going home!" the old man added as he whisked his companion away.

Nahshon approached Ellis as he pondered at the edge of the overlook. He could feel the breeze from the wind going against his face, the direction that the hat should have gone.

"Ellis, I did it."

"Yes, you did," Ellis replied.

As the two stood there at the edge of the overlook, Ellis turned to look straight at Nahshon with an expression of pride on his face.

"And so much more. There's a lot of things just now that I've noticed other than making it go the other direction. You're a marvel,

Nahshon. And check out your nose…It's not bleeding. You're getting stronger, son."

Nahshon ran his finger across his nostrils and noticed the lack of blood on it. He felt a sense of accomplishment with the results of the feat he just performed.

"I want to keep going, Ellis. I want to continue getting stronger," Nahshon said.

"Nahshon, tell me, what is the earliest recollection that you have of your abilities?"

"I remember seeing things when I was a small child, but it's all so sketchy in my mind. Dammit, I wish I could remember," Nahshon replied in frustration.

"Maybe we can do something about that…"

"We can?" asked Nahshon.

"We can try, but I want you to do me a favor and rest the remainder of the evening. I want you to come over to my apartment tomorrow, and we'll figure this out together," Ellis responded.

Nahshon nodded his head in agreement.

"This park really does have a beautiful overlook of the city," Nahshon said as the two turned to look outward over the overlook.

"It really does. I never really took notice of it until today," Ellis smiled as he replied.

CHAPTER 12

Nahshon tried to get some good sleep, but it became impossible. The idea of getting to the bottom of why his strange and unusual perspective had been with him most of his life and the prospect of learning to master it was too good an offer to resist.

As he stood outside of Ellis's door, his mind drifted to the collection of users that tried to exploit him and his abilities including Dr. Reed Richardson. How maybe he could finally understand why it is that these variations of numbers exploded out of his mind and fate bent at their will. Ellis was very adamant about him being there at that specific time and not arriving late, which also caused Nahshon to wonder, but it was time to come in and get the process starting, so Nahshon knocked twice on the door.

"Nahshon! Hey, come on in," Ellis said as he opened the door to invite his young friend in.

"Ellis, I can't tell you how excited I am to get down to business. I tried to do what you said, but I gotta be honest I really didn't get as much sleep as I probably should have."

"No worries. We'll make do with what we got," responded Ellis as he hung Nahshon's jacket up on the rack.

"I gotta tell you. I can't wait to find out how—"

"Actually that part can wait, Nahshon," Ellis interjected. "First, it's the weekend. Let's chill and watch football games on TV. Take your pick: the couch or the recliner," Ellis added as he waited for Nahshon's response.

"Okay…the recliner?" said a puzzled Nahshon.

"Cool. I'll take the couch," Ellis responded as he went into the kitchen to bring in some snacks for them to enjoy the game with.

An hour had passed as the two were watching the football game on television when Nahshon started to figure out that there was a method to Ellis's madness. He insisted on watching a football game first in order to put the two of them in a more comfortable state. Also by watching a complete football game, it would subconsciously ease Nahshon from dwelling on what happened in the Galinsky game and witness what happened when something did go according to plan.

Nahshon smirked at the gesture Ellis had taken, and though he recognized Ellis's intention, he nonetheless appreciated the fact that he cared enough to do it. After the fourth quarter ended and the players on the field were making their way back to the locker rooms, Nahshon propped himself up in the recliner and glanced over at Ellis.

"How do you feel, Nahshon?" asked Ellis.

"Great."

"Good…then let's begin," responded Ellis.

Ellis got up from the couch and reached for the remote to turn the TV off. He then went over to the switch for his ceiling lights and dimmed them to a comfortable and relaxed illumination. When Nahshon started to get up to go to the couch, Ellis gestured for him to remain where he was, reassuring him where he sat was exactly where he needed to be.

"Nahshon, I'm going to attempt to get you to reach back and recall your earliest recollections of when your abilities manifested themselves."

"How are you going to do that?" Nahshon asked.

"Just relax. I'm going to use a method called regression hypnotherapy, otherwise known as regression to cause. We're going to try to establish a bridge to certain past events leading to something substantial to anchor ourselves to and pinpoint the emergence of your abilities."

"Okay. I get it," replied Nahshon.

"Nahshon, before we begin, I have to warn you. What you relive could be unpleasant, like many bad memories are. Some might be traumatic. If that's something you want to avoid, then we can go back to the drawing board, and I'll do more research to find another way," Ellis said.

"I understand, Ellis. And I'm ready for whatever it is we need to do," Nahshon replied courageously.

"Okay then," said Ellis.

Ellis got Nahshon to relax and sit back into the recliner. The lights were dim, and as his feet were extended up from the recliner, Nahshon felt himself getting more relaxed and a bit drowsy. Ellis instructed Nahshon to go through an exercise of relaxed and controlled breathing. Soon Nahshon felt as if he was drifting off into slumber while still fully attentive of what Ellis was saying.

"Nahshon? Can you hear me?" Ellis said in a low calm voice.

"Yes, I can," answered Nahshon.

"Good. I want you to reach back into your mind past our meeting and pass your first meeting with Reed Richardson. Do you recall the name of the last person to abuse you and your abilities before you met Reed Richardson?"

There was a stillness as Nahshon reached back into the recesses of his mind until a name came bursting out from his past.

"Phin," Nahshon replied as a disturbed grimace appeared on his face. "Phineas Knox."

"Can you tell me about Phineas, Nahshon?" Ellis inquired.

"Well, for one thing, he hated that he was called Phineas. It reminded him of how uneducated a person he was to have such an astute name as Phineas. He became my foster parent when I was about thirteen. He told the agency that the reason he wanted to become a foster parent was that the love of his life died, and without a child, he felt the emptiness of not being a father. Being a father to a child was the one great accomplishment that he wanted in life. Of course, they bought that crock of crap and gave him me as his foster child.

"At first things seemed cool, almost like a big brother-little brother relationship. He had a girlfriend named Dawn, who would frequent his house. She was very nice to me, and the living arrangement seemed like a decent one. That was, of course, until the day he had friends over to watch a whole day of football games. At some time during the first matchup, one of his friends asked me to guess who the winner would be. I did, and the team that I chose made everyone laugh. The team that I picked was predicted to get slaughtered by the odds-on favorite.

"Phineas and his friends thought I got lucky at first, but to humor himself, one of his friends asked me to look at all the matchups in the newspaper and circle which teams I thought would win. As I looked on the page with the logo of the teams that were facing each other, I noticed one of the teams having a greenish hue around it, and one would have a reddish hue.

"That told me that the one with the greenish hue would probably be the winner and the reddish-hued team logo would be the loser. I circled the winners and handed the newspaper back to Phineas's friend. Another one of his friends mocked me, and I stormed off away to my room.

"Later that evening, I was sitting on my bed listening to my headphones when Phineas stormed in and grabbed the headphone set and tossed it before I could say anything. I felt his hands grab the back of my neck in a viselike grip, and he jerked my head down almost toward my knees. The pain in the back of my neck felt almost as if he was trying to crush my spine.

"He yelled at me that I had embarrassed him around his friends and that I had been holding out on him on how I could pick winning teams. He said that every last one of my picks came out right, and he was ridiculed by his friends for not using me to help him make money.

"He forced me to reveal how I've was able to tell who was going to win, and I admitted to him about the aura I was able to see when I looked on the paper. Though listening to me, he didn't truly believe me. He started to think it over, and his grip start to loosen at the back of my neck.

"He sat down next to me and gave a fake apology to manhandling me and that he needed my help in order for us to have a better living situation. I was too afraid to question him, so I nodded my head in agreement.

"The following weekend me, Phin and his girlfriend, Dawn, made a road trip to the local casino. While Phin was inside, I sat in the car with Dawn in the casino parking lot, in contact with him by cell phone. I would look at the paper and dictate to Dawn what teams appeared greenish, and she would relay it back to Phin to place his bets.

"The operation worked like a charm, and I made a lot of good money for them, but the more we won, the more Phin got greedy and made me use my abilities to pick bets for him. It was beginning to cause a strain on me, and the headaches and nosebleeds start increasing. I could tell Dawn was a little sympathetic, but she was too afraid to say anything to Phineas for fear that she might receive some his abuse.

"One day my body had hit a wall, and I simply could not see any auras on the newspaper. It was like my abilities had shut down for repairs. I pushed myself too far, and I didn't know how long it would take until I was able to access it again.

"When I couldn't provide Phin with my predictions, he tried to do it himself, and he risked a lot of money on some of his bets. When he returned to the car a few hours later, he banged on the car door window. Both Dawn and myself had fallen asleep waiting on him all that time, and when she unhooked the locks, he rushed to my door and yanked it open and pulled me out to the parking lot pavement.

"He stood over me with his knee in my chest, pinning me down, fuming about losing all his money and how it was all my fault. I tried to tell him that I could not see anything anymore and that I was too exhausted to try again. That enraged him, and he balled his fists and started punching me over and over again in my face. He took a minute to pause, and I looked over at Dawn for help with calming him down so that he would get off me, but she was too afraid to help and looked away.

"He continued assaulting me, and the punches turned into a choking as he vented his frustration at me for losing all his money. I thought I was going die at this grown man's hands, but there was something he saw in my eyes that caused him to stop and back away, almost in fear.

"He yelled at me to get back in the car and slammed the door behind me once I got in. We drove away from the casino. On the way back to his house, not a word was said. Dawn continued to look out the window, too ashamed to look in her mirror back at me and too afraid to say something to Phin.

"That night I snuck out of the house and ran away. I knew I couldn't go back to the abuse that Phin was giving me. A friend I had made at the school I was at asked his parents if I could stay with them. When I told them about the abuse I was experiencing, they made a call to children's services, and I was permanently removed from Phineas Knox's home. I stayed a couple weeks at my friend's house and then I was returned to the group home. I never knew what happened to Dawn, but I hope she was okay."

Nahshon paused as he rubbed the back of his neck, an obvious indication that reliving the trauma suffered at the hands of his former foster father had a lasting effect.

Ellis's heart broke hearing the sad story that Nahshon told, but he knew it was necessary to keep going on with the process of unraveling locked memories that the young man had. Without changing his tone, he continued on with his questioning.

"Now, Nahshon, we're going to leave Phineas Knox and go deeper into the past, more and more years before. I want you to reach back and try to remember the first time that you recall using your abilities for someone. Maybe it's a name or a certain face or maybe even a smell," Ellis said.

"A smell...a smell...More like a stench...like the stench of Newport cigarettes," Nahshon replied in a trancelike tone.

"When I was around seven, I had a foster mother by the name of Kristin Alexander. Ms. Kristin was very skinny and frail and always wore clothing to show it. I was too young to recognize it. Now I can honestly say that she was a hoarder. I think she had a husband that left her and her natural kids, but I guess, like most hoarders, two were not enough, so she began hoarding children as a foster mother. Even though she was able to portray a stable home to the caseworkers, the reality was that the house was full of filth and trash among other things. Along with myself were two other foster children. One was black, and the other one was, I think, Hispanic. She would go around people she knew and called the lot of us her 'Rainbow Tribe Even though people thought that she was this sweet caregiver to a bunch of kids, the reality was she was very cold and abusive to us since we were foster kids of color. I remember she always called us racial slurs. I was so young I didn't know yet what a miserable situation it was. It was all that I had, and the children that I live with was very nice to me even though Ms. Kristin was not. I guess you could say we had each other to lean on.

"One day we were in a grocery store. Ms. Kristin was trying to get her daily fix of scratch offs. Ms. Kristin had a very bad problem with the throwing her money away on scratch offs and lotteries. Sometimes her addiction for gambling would result in us not having much food to eat. Some of us kids grabbed some candy with the hopes that she would add them along with her scratch offs, which she usually didn't.

"With a bag of M&Ms, I looked up at the counter, and on the rack was a dispenser of scratch-off tickets. The dispenser on the left had a strange greenish aura around. While I was looking at the dispenser, Ms. Kristin was asking the clerk for her usual pack of Newports. As I was staring at the dispenser, I yelled out, 'That one!' drawing Ms. Kristin's attention toward me.

"At first, she looked infuriated at me for drawing her attention, but when she saw the conviction in my face for what I was staring at, she knew that there was something going on. She asked me what was it, and when I pointed and told her that was the one, she tore off some of the scratch-offs from the dispenser and laid them on the table.

"She asked me again which one of the six scratch-offs that she had on the counter was the one I wanted, and I pointed to the second one—its greenish hue was more visible to me. She purchased that scratch-off, much to the chagrin of the clerk, who saw her tear off the other ones, and she used the coin in her pocket to scratch it off right then and there. The scratch-off was a winner for $60, and

Ms. Kristin was elated. She leaned down to and whispered if I saw any more I liked. I looked at the dispenser again, and in the roll was another greenish scratch-off and nodded my head to her.

"She winded up spending roughly twenty bucks on scratch, also including the ones that she tore off previously to get to the one I was looking at. When she purchased it and scratched it off, it was a $50 winner, and she was excited again. She had just made a total of $90 from her scratch-offs and received her cash directly from the ticked-off clerk. The angry clerk refused to let her continue, so she rounded us kids up and for the first time, bought all of us to candy that we wanted and took us back home. That was a good day.

"This started a pattern with Ms. Kristin and myself where she would take me to the different stores that she knew had scratch-offs and run a routine of me pointing out to her which were the winners. Even though she only took me and left the other kids back home I would insist that she get us all some candy because I really liked the other kids, and I didn't want them to be left out.

"Her habit of using me to point out winning scratch-offs got out of hand, and the conditions around the house got even worse. Not to mention she had a drug habit, and with more money coming in, her ability to feed it increased. We all could tell that she was on something, but we were little kids and too afraid to say something.

"One day she came in with a brand-new dress for going out, with the store plastic draping over it. There was barely anything to eat at the house, and her daughter, the oldest among us, had to scrap some leftovers together for us five kids to eat. She seemed very excited but was still inattentive to us kids and our needs. After two hours of her being in a room, she resurfaced and put on some noodles for us to eat as she kept puffing away on her Newport cigarettes.

"That evening, she called me over to sit next to her. I had an uneasy feeling about it. Her eyes seemed a little glazed, and she was uncommonly friendly towards me. As I sat next to her, the smoke from the ashtray of her lit Newport rose up into my face, and I could breathe in that putrid smell that I was really growing to hate.

"I watched her pull out a stack of lottery tickets which she laid out on the glass table. One by one she spread them all across until you could barely see the glass of the table. Next she told me to pick the winner. I wasn't sure what she meant by her question, so I didn't say anything. She repeated herself again, and again I looked at her in confusion. She took her index finger loudly on the table, ordering me to pick which one would be winner.

"She yelled at me as to why I didn't see it. All I could tell her was I did not know. The other two foster kids and her youngest heard the commotion and backed off into their room. There was a tense stare down between me and her, she being irate whereas I was just bewildered. She told me to do what I do and find the winner, and I told her I couldn't because I didn't know how to.

"Just then the state lottery came on the television, and she stopped yelling at me. She gathered herself and paid close attention to the lottery show host reading off the lucky numbers. I tried to get up off the couch, but she ordered me to stay put. As the numbers were being read, she panicked and shuffled through all the lottery tickets on the table looking for a match. As she was doing that, she kept yelling at me to 'do something.' All I could do was watch her fail at winning the lottery.

"As the lottery broadcast ended, I watched her shuffle through all the tickets hoping she might've misread them and that one of them was the winner. I was afraid, so I started to get up, but she grabbed me by my arms and started shaking me. She called me a 'stupid little Nigger' and blamed me for her losing all her money on those lottery tickets and the clothes she came home with.

"I told her I was sorry, even though I didn't know what I was sorry for, but she wasn't trying to hear it. She looked over at her ashtray and saw one of her Newport still lit in it. She took the lit cigarette and started to burn my arm over and over with it. I could feel that lasting painful sting each time she burned into my arm, making me scream like crazy.

"I begged her to stop, but she would not listen until she completely put the cigarette out on the flesh of my arm. All the while she was punishing me, that disgusting smell of those Newports rose up into my nose."

Ellis silently watched as Nahshon's arm reached over to rub along the arm that he'd been burned on, stroking it as if it happened recently. It was easy for Ellis to realize that this childhood trauma was something that Nahshon carried with him for very long time. He wanted to comfort his young friend, but he remained silent and let him continue on.

"Eventually she got too enraged to stand the sight of me, and she stormed off back into her room. I used that opportunity to run away from the couch and back into the room with the other kids. The rest of the night was spent with some of the younger kids comforting me and putting cool towels on my arm while Ms. Kristin spent the remaining night laid out in her room on drugs.

"That next morning, there was a banging on the door that woke everyone in the house up, and when Ms. Kristin open the door, police and people from child services stormed in. They were responding to an anonymous call that was made of abuse going on in the home and were sent to investigate it. Some of the people from children's services came into our bedroom and got us dressed and out of there while the police searched Ms. Kristin's room, only to discover some of her drug paraphernalia.

"While we were standing outside with the child services people, the police led out Ms. Kristin in handcuffs. Right before they put her in their police car, she stared face-to-face with her oldest daughter, obviously figuring out that the teenager was the one who made the anonymous call. After that we were sent to different group homes. I never heard of Ms. Kristin again or the other foster kids. They were good kids. I hope they ended up well…"

"So much pain for someone so young," Ellis said. "That's not how childhood memories should be. A childhood should be filled with fond memories. Playful memories full of laughter, joy, games, color, and music."

"Music, but I do remember…Music…Music like a melody… The melody of a song. Wait, I have another memory…I remember her singing. I remember my mother."

Ellis propped himself up from the couch and locked his fingers to his chin in deep thought. A breakthrough was reached, and he needed to probe more.

"That's good, Nahshon. You're doing it. You're delving deeper. Tell me about your mother."

"She was young and beautiful, but there was sadness in her face. I could look up, and for a second, you could see the sad expression she had quickly changed into smiles to conceal it. She loved music, and when she would feel sad or angry, she always sang her favorite song that always made her feel better. Sometimes she would sing it fast like it was supposed to be, but every now and then, she would slow it down, and it almost sound like a lullaby.

"She would hold my hand so tight and let me walk along with her when I was able to. I always felt loved by her. I remember she didn't like the sound of my cry, and she would be rushing to console me in order to make it stop, and I loved that about her. She never let me be sad for long."

"That's a beautiful memory Nahshon. Tell me about the last time you saw her."

"We were walking together along the street She was yelling at some woman a few minutes before, and her grip was a little tighter than usual, but I remember her fingers rubbing against my hand and her grip loosened.

"She stopped our walking to kneel down in front of me to say, 'One way or another, we're going to be okay.' All I could do was smile back. I loved her so. She stood back up, and we continued walking along the street. Her pace picked up, and she had more cheerful step about her, and I remember she began singing her favorite song once more:

I'm the ruler of my destiny
If I fall then it's because of me
There is nobody who's got the power
To determine what becomes of me
I'm aware of what we're here to do
And, do is our only choice
And if you like it'll be ME and YOU

"She would always put a little something extra when she said 'me and you' while our arms swayed back and forth as she looked down at me.

"When I lifted my head up and looked ahead down the block, suddenly I could see a red mass all the way at the end, and I felt a sickness in my stomach.

"I stopped in my footsteps, and my mother looked down at me, asking what was the matter. I was so young and I didn't have the vocabulary yet to tell her that I could see something bad down the horizon. She was in a hurry wherever we were going, and she assured me everything would be okay, so we continued walking in the direction of the object. While we were walking, a man passed by. He didn't look that old. He looked around my mom's age, and as he passed, they both looked back at each other. There's something about the man's ring that caught my eye. It was a golden ring that had an animal inscribed on it that made it really shine. Maybe it was the sunlight."

Nahshon's breathing start to increase as if he was beginning to hyperventilate, and his voice had a whimper. The more he spoke, the more uncomfortable he became.

"We got to the end of the block and…and…I stopped again, preventing us from starting to cross the street. My mother turned around to once again ask me what was wrong, but she didn't know that the red moving mass was floating around behind her in the background.

"She assured me one more time that there was nothing to be afraid of and that we would walk together across the crosswalk. She was already partially standing in the street and the corner when she spoke to me and, and as she turned around to step into the street, it was like the red mass swallowed her up in one moment and her hand was pulled away from my hand. It was so fast.

"I felt myself moving forward into the street, but a hand grabbed me by my shoulder and another hand took hold of my waist and pulled me back. I could hear people screaming around me, and as I looked up, I saw that it was the man who my mother looked back at. The man with the bird inscribed on his ring."

"'Ring'?" responded Ellis.

Just then Ellis's front door was kicked in as Reed and two other men in helmets and gear came rushing in. One of the men took out a Taser and fired it into Nahshon's chest before he could come out of his hypnosis. The sudden shock of the volts rendered him unconscious.

As Ellis leaped off the couch, the other man brandished his Taser and fired it at Ellis, striking him above his chest near his collarbone. The volts coursed through him, and he made a quick shout. Everything in his body went limp, and he crashed down into the floor.

The man that Tasered Nahshon rushed to him and covered his head with a sack and tightened it around his neck. He also cuffed his hands behind his back and hoisted him up to carry him outside. Ellis tried again to move toward Nahshon, but additional volts was sent through the Taser, shocking him back to immobility.

"Reed…," Ellis grunted as he was wracked with pain on the floor.

"Some doors are best left unopened, Ellis. All I asked you to do was to probe him a little, get a better understanding of his abilities. But I knew you would make it an obsession and that you would bring everything out. And you've done a very good job of it. Better than I ever could.

"But did you really think that you were getting one over on me? That you were capable of withholding information about Nahshon?" Reed said as he leaned closer over Ellis's prone body on the floor.

"We had you bugged ever since the incident that happened at the Galinsky game. Why look so surprised? Of course I knew that was Nahshon's doing and that you two would bond following the manifestation of his powers. Here. Your office. Inside your car. You been bugged everywhere," Reed said as he pulled Ellis's head back to look into his eyes. "Because he's that important."

"And I know you, always having a bleeding heart. And I feel for you. After everything that happened to your son. But I had faith in you, and I knew you could bring it somehow out of Nahshon. The problem is you cannot look at this…person…as if he's a surrogate son to replace Grant. He is so much more than he looks, and we have to have him."

Reed stood up from Ellis and strolled to the helmeted man holding the Taser. He stared for second at the stoically silent man and then turned back around to Ellis.

"These men here wanted to kill you. In fact, they still want to kill you. But I don't want that, Ellis. I still consider you my friend. So because of that, you're being allowed to live. But I have to warn you: *don't come for him.* Or you will lose so much more than you expected."

"Reed…don't do this. He's been through enough," uttered Ellis.

"Oh, I know. We heard the whole story. Very tragic. Very sad. He's had more hardships than most men like us. But I can't do anything about that for him. Not with the untapped potential he possesses," Reed replied as he adjusted his jacket.

"Remember what I said, Ellis. *Let this one go.* You have an amazing talent for getting to the bottom of things with people, and there are plenty of more people that you can help. This one you have to let go. And I'm truly sorry, I know this is the end of our friendship. But I'm truly sorry. Goodbye, old friend," said Reed as he turned around toward the front door.

Ellis lifted his head up from the floor, which was met by the blunt end of the gun against the back of his head. Everything in his view turned to shadow as his eyes closed and he succumbed to the darkness of unconsciousness.

CHAPTER 13

The dank air filled his nostrils, going down his airways to the base of his throat, forcing him to cough. Each cough made him remember the sensations in his body, and he realized that he could move again. As his eyes opened, they were still met by darkness, not the complete darkness that comes when your eyes close but almost a grayish black tent that can only come with having something over your head.

Nahshon tried to move his arms, but he realized that he was bound from behind. At the same time he became aware of his arms, he realized that he could not stand up and was in fact lying down. It was then, in that moment of dread, that he made the conclusion that he was trapped somewhere as a prisoner.

As more sensations became evident, he realized by the constant rocking and humming sound beneath him that he was in motion, most likely inside a car. His next realization was that the limited space he felt himself cramped in could only be the space provided by the inside of the trunk. His next thought was, What had happened to his friend Ellis? Was he alive? Was he dead? What had happened to him?

As he gained a measure of composure, his mind raced on how he could get out of the captivity that he was in. First, he would need to get his sight back to see how he would be able to escape. He had to create an opening in whatever was over his head to see. Nahshon started scraping his head around the floor of the enclosed area until he felt something with an edge to it.

He began rubbing the surface of the cloth over his head against the edgy object, and a scraping sound was made. He continued over and over again with the scraping until he began to notice a lightness in the view from inside the cloth; the fabric was giving way. As he theorized, a tear was being made in the fabric. After a while, the tearing continued, and a beam of lightness creeped through the fabric and met his eyes.

He had torn a slight hole in his covering, and he exploited it by pushing his head against the slit, making the tear in the fabric begin to grow. Nahshon got more anxious as his face was making its way through the fabric. At last the fabric tore enough for his head to escape through, and the remainder of the cloth slinked down to his neck.

The light that he thought was so luminous as he was tearing his way through the bag over his head was not that much different from the darkness of the trunk. Nahshon looked around in the cramped area for something that gave off any semblance of light. As he scanned the floor of the trunk, he noticed that there was a slit of corrosion, and upon close inspection, he could see something moving from the outside of the vehicle.

Also in the trunk with him was a tire iron, which was close by his head. Nahshon nudged his head on top of the tire iron and pushed it toward himself slowly. Carefully he nudged the tire iron toward the spot with the corrosive cut in the floor. When he got the tire iron to partly lay over the corrosive slit, he pressed his head on top of the tire, rubbing it along the tear slowly and painfully.

Nahshon rubbed the tire iron along the cut until the tip of the tire iron made its way into the tear in the floor. Nahshon continued going over the tire iron with his head, forcing it to widen the space of the tear. Nahshon smiled at his small accomplishment and then continued his efforts. Eventually the tear in the floor became a hole as the tire iron completely fell through and made a noise along the ground.

Nahshon gasped and then remained still and silent, terrified that the noise made would make his captors stop the vehicle and come back to inspect the trunk. The vehicle continued on its course uninterrupted, which gave Nahshon a sigh of relief that they didn't notice the tire iron falling out from the bottom. The space that was created in the floor now resembled a hole from which Nahshon could see the sight of moving road.

The terrain that the vehicle was moving on changed, and it caused the vehicle as a whole to move more intensely. Wherever they were, it was obvious that the vehicle was going uphill. Nahshon knew that if there was any way he could escape, it had to be now.

Nahshon shifted his head to look at the inside of the trunk. He heard it rattling before as he moved around and figured that if it was rattling, then something in it must be loose. As his eyes fixated on the lock, he began to think about Ellis. His memory went to the park when Ellis tasked him to focus his abilities:

> "The wind is blowing in her face. She's in the same direction as we are. You can tell by it blowing her hat backward?"
> "Right. I want to see you try to make her hat fly off in the opposite direction of the wind."
> "What! That's impossible!"
> "Not for you. I believe in you, Nahshon. Try it."

Nahshon closed his eyes and thought to himself, *What are the chances of the locking mechanism in this trunk being loose?"* then he opened his eyes and focused his stare at the inside lock. Numbers began to appear around the inside lock mechanism, and Nahshon increased his focus.

The numbers that were reddish began to decrease in value as the greenish numbers' amounts began to increase. As the green numbers began rising, Ellis could hear the sound of something moving within the lock, and when the vehicle came upon a pronounced bump, a click could be heard as the trunk itself wobbled, showing a slight bit of sunshine briefly passing in. Nahshon felt like he'd succeeded.

Next, Nahshon lay his head along the floor of the truck next to the hole that the tire iron had created. He stared at the outside of the vehicle, along the ground, watching a blur go by as occasional rocks pelted the bottom of the vehicle. At the same time, he extended his legs as best he could up against the inner wall of the truck, as if bracing himself for an impact.

As the side of his head lay next to the hole, he closed his eyes once more and thought to himself *What are the chances of the biggest hardest rock on the road hitting the bottom of this vehicle?* And then he opened his eyes and stared down at the moving road. Once again a variety of numbers appeared in both red and green.

Nahshon's focus was complicated by the blur of the moving road underneath him. At first, the numbers didn't change much, and doubt began to set in, but he drew upon the words his friend had given him, and he doubled his efforts to concentrate. Nahshon could feel blood starting to flow from his nostril down to the side of his face. The strain was intense, but he was beginning to see the green numbers starting to increase in value. One of the numbers in particular was entering in the 90s, and Nahshon focused on that one—*94, 95, 96, 97, 98.*

Nahshon braced himself once more. This was the first time that he'd ever used his ability to aid himself, and he didn't know what would happen with the actions he was trying to create. Whatever was going to happen was going to cause some trouble to the vehicle, and it probably was going to hurt.

Reed sat in the back seat, mulling over the betrayal he had given his friend of over twenty years while playing with a set of keys in his hand. Nothing was said in the car ride as the two helmeted men rolled in the front seats. There wasn't much that could be said between the three of them; they were there to provide any muscle that he needed for his task, and they got the job done. As Reed began to stare outside the window, a huge rock collided underneath their car, rocking the car slightly to its side.

"Holy shit!" Reed yelled as the impact of the rocking car forced him to the door on the other side.

As the rock collided with the muffler underneath the car and violently jolted the vehicle, the impact catapulted Nahshon's back against the trunk door. The loose locking mechanism gave way, and the impact knocked Nahshon out of the still moving car. Nahshon's shoulders crashed onto the ground as he began rolling. His arms were still handcuffed behind him, so he couldn't catch himself with his hands. As he kept rolling, he went down the side of the hill from the road that the car was driving.

As Reed recovered himself in his seat, he looked behind him to see the trunk door swinging upward in full view.

"The trunk's open! Damn it, stop the car!" Reed yelled to the two men in front.

The car stopped, and the three men ran out toward the back of the vehicle. Reed arrived first and to his horror, found that Nahshon was not there. The three men looked all around in bewilderment, perplexed as to where he had fallen down at.

"Oh, Jesus! We gotta look around for him. He couldn't have gotten far. Wait…Get back in the car. We gotta go back downhill to grab him!" Reed said.

But it was too late. Nahshon was already rolling down the hill from below. The descent wasn't steep, however, due to mudslides caused by the constant rain around that area. With his hand still handcuffed behind his back, Nahshon could not grab or grip to slow his descent downward. It was almost as if he was on some wet slide except for the occasional bump into sediment rocks.

As he burrowed down farther and farther down the hill, he could look far ahead into the horizon and see that it would lead to a peak that would send him in the air toward the ground below. As his eyes looked beyond, he could see there was a highway underneath the horde of passing cars. It was then that Nahshon panicked, realizing that he would be sent spiraling toward incoming traffic.

He tried frantically to grab some of the ground, but it was too damp and he was going down too fast. It seemed like the longer the descent, the faster his speed picked up. Even in the grasp of imminent danger, his mind drifted to the last image of his mother when she stepped off the curb as the oncoming bus tragically plowed into her before his very eyes.

"No!" he cried out in a panicked scream.

As Nahshon's eyes glared ahead at the freeway approaching, it was engulfed in a sea of red color and variables of numbers. Nahshon focused on the center of the mass in his view, and suddenly the numbers started changing and lowering in its value as a blotch of green coloration started forming. The greenish blotch started to grow, and the numbers within it started increasing. Eventually, in his view, the greenish area had plowed its way to the center of the mass of red color surrounding the freeway.

Forcefully the slide down ended as Nahshon hit the cliff and was jettisoned into the air toward the oncoming traffic. He was helpless to even try to shield himself. Nahshon's body flipped forward, still bound behind his hands.

Just then a cargo truck passed by and went through the exact spot where the green blotch in Nahshon's view was at the exact moment of his fall. Nahshon crashed right on top of the moving truck into the center of its trailer. Somehow the force of his landing made the handcuffs strike a part of the trailer and broke its mechanism, releasing one of the cuffs.

The trailer of the truck had a crafted indent on the top which resembled somewhat like a ditch for something the size of a large object or person could fit in. As the truck continued down the freeway, it passed an opening area where a car pulled to the side was with men standing outside. It was Reed and his accomplices looking around the area for Nahshon to turn up from his fall downhill. The truck went right past Reed with his back turned, and Nahshon nestled in the nook at the top of the trailer. Reed was totally oblivious to Nahshon slipping past him.

Nahshon sat up and turned around as he rubbed his bruised wrist, one of which still had the broken handcuff attached to it. As he looked forward on top of the truck, he could see the sign for an exit containing a truck rest stop only one mile ahead. The speed of the truck start decreasing as if it was preparing to get on the exit, and

Nahshon figured that the rest stop was where the truck was heading. There would be the opportunity for him to get down once it parked.

As he sat there continually rubbing his wrists, Nahshon no longer had any doubt on how the safe landing from falling down the hill had occurred. He'd made it happen. His subconscious desire to avoid repeating the same fate as his mother caused him to use his abilities. He was growing stronger and more powerful. But for now he needed to make sure he was safely away from his captors and to make sure his dear friend Ellis was safe.

He felt a throbbing pain in his left foot and realized that he had injured it somehow in the collision within the trunk that ejected him out of his captors' car. As his adrenaline was starting to wane, the pain in his foot increased, letting him know that it would be a problem.

But for now, he lay back down in the nook of the trailer to gather himself and be ready to press forward once the truck came to its rest stop.

CHAPTER 14

The thunderclap pounding throughout your skull is intense. There's a soreness around the rings of your eyes as the muscles around them start to flinch. Followed by a heaviness in your eyelids as you force them to raise up to meet the light around you. You force yourself to swallow, which has a certain pain to it because you haven't done so for a long time.

Most of the muscles in your body ache from the ordeal it has gone through, especially the neck, which had stayed in the same position for quite a while. As your eyes try to focus at its blurry surroundings, your eyelash mingle with the fibers of the carpet. The body resents the effort that you are putting up and longs to shut itself down and returned to the slumber you came from. But you know that this is not the state that you were supposed to be in, and you fire up your will to return you to coherent consciousness.

This is what Ellis felt as he pulled himself up from the floor where he was left. As he slowly sat up, he could feel the ache in the back of his head and ran his fingers along the source of its pain, only to notice the blood on his fingers. It was most likely the area that he was struck at that caused his blackout. He glanced down at the rug where his head lay and saw some of the blood from his head blended in with the color of his rug.

"Dammit, Reed. Why?" Ellis muttered as he continued stroking the back of his wounded head.

As Ellis tried to prop himself up against the couch, he became woozy and fell back into the cushion of the couch. He realized that there was still some disorientation from either the blow to his head or the shock to his system from the Taser or both.

"Damn. They got Nahshon," Ellis said as he rubbed his temples with his head sunk low in despair.

Ellis realized that it wasn't like how he had always believed in the movies. Usually the protagonists immediately recover from being unconscious and can go take charge to stop the villain. The movies never mentioned how the hero can barely stand on his own two feet and take a couple of steps.

The clarity of the situation started becoming clearer in Ellis's mind, and he knew that time was of the essence to try and find his young friend. He forced himself up and took a couple steps while his arms used various surrounding furniture as a crutch. Eventually his legs began to strengthen, and the rest of his body returned to keeping him upright.

With every step, his mind began to assess what actions took place during his unconsciousness and what his former friend and colleague could have taken from him. As he surveyed the area around them, he didn't notice anything overturned or scattered as if someone ravaged his condo, but he remembered his case files and private notes about Nahshon that he had left in his file cabinet in the bedroom.

As Ellis entered his bedroom, his suspicions turned out to be correct—Reed had been in his file cabinet and stolen his files on Nahshon. He shuffled through his file cabinet, hoping that there might be something on Nahshon that Reed could have missed. But when he realized everything was taken, he slammed the door shut in disgust.

Ellis returned to his living room and sat in one his chairs as he tried to brainstorm Reed's motives and where he might have taken Nahshon. He thought about how he could try and find Reed when a sudden thought came about him, and he reached into his back pocket of his jeans.

"Thank God they didn't get my phone from me," he said.

As luck would have it, Ellis figured by his positioning on the floor that he happened to be lying on the pocket that housed his phone. Since they were in a hurry to get out of there with Nahshon and the files, checking him for his phone was not on their minds. He picked up his phone and made a call out to the center to see if they had heard from Reed. He calmed his speaking voice so that he could sound more professional on the call.

"Wakefield Center for Youth Intervention and Behavioral Treatment. My name is Trisha. Can I help you?"

"Um, yes. Hello, Trisha, this is Dr. Ellis Daniels calling. I'm trying to get a hold of Dr. Reed Richardson. We're supposed to have a dinner engagement this evening, and I was trying to get in contact with him for confirmation," Ellis replied.

"Oh! Hello, Dr. Daniels. I'm sorry, there hasn't been any messages from Dr. Richardson at the desk. However, I'm looking at the vacations board, and it has him down as blocking a week of vacation off that started yesterday. He didn't mention it to you?"

"Maybe he did, and I simply forgot. Been a rough couple of weeks with my hectic schedule. Too much on my mind these days. He probably told me and went in one ear and out the other," Ellis jested as he answered the receptionist's questions.

"I understand, sir. Should I leave him a message?"

"No, that won't be necessary. I'll try calling him on his personal phone. Thank you, Trisha," Ellis responded.

"No problem, Dr. Daniels. Bye-bye."

Ellis pressed the button on his phone to end the call. The expression on his face reverted back to the reality of his feelings at the moment.

"Reed, where are you taking Nahshon that you need to travel to…" Ellis said as he began to theorize Reed's motives.

Ellis knew that he needed to act quickly. He went to his key rack to get his car keys so that he could at least get on the road, but to no avail. He found the rack bare.

"He took my car keys," Ellis said to himself.

After that Ellis ventured outside to his car to hopefully find some way to try and hotwire the ignition. As he got closer to the vehicle, he realized that all the tires had been slashed. Reed had made sure that his pursuit would be derailed.

"Well, Reed, I never figured you for a dullard," Ellis said.

Ellis slowly walked back into his condo and sat down in one of his chairs, rubbing his fingers again on the spot on his head where he was struck. There was a feeling of disbelief at all that transpired and the betrayal of someone who was once one of his oldest friends.

He took a deep breath and sighed, trying to calm his nerves as his mind reached back to the early days of he and Reed's friendship. The idea that he would reach to such lengths to exploit someone was telling of how far they had fallen.

He dove back to the early days when he was in grad school psychology and how he was new to the city and the first person he met was another young grad student also from out of state. The friendship was established early from long nights of cramming for exams and girl watching. They both hailed from relatively small towns, so it was an exciting time to be young and on your own. It was also frightening too.

But the two of them eventually got more comfortable in their surrounding as well as grad school and eventually gained some other friends. They got along so well they decided to be roommates to save money. They enjoyed using their place as the epicenter for a host of poker nights and Super Bowl parties.

Their poker nights, in particular, were epic, with lots of highlights to mark the nights. There were many arguments, jokes, and wild stories to cap off the night. Reed, in particular, made poker his obsession, sometimes making very costly wages that sometimes jeopardized his half of the finance of their apartment. Ellis wouldn't say much, but he could tell that his friend was showing signs of a gambling addiction.

Right before they graduated, they both met the women who would eventually be their wives around the same time, and they also became fast friends. They would do couples vacations together and spend nights out with each other.

After graduation, they both landed their first postcollege jobs at different organizations, but they still kept in touch. They both got serious in their relationships with Dana and Reed's girlfriend, Nancy, and Ellis was honored to be asked by Reed to be one of his grooms-men at his wedding. Ellis followed suit a year later and had Reed in his wedding party when he married Dana.

As luck would have it, both Nancy and Dana discovered that they were pregnant around the same time. It was almost as if the cou-ples were destined to do everything together. Unfortunately for Reed and Nancy, she miscarried in her second trimester. Dana's pregnancy continued without any difficulty, and Grant was born. The Daniels were there for Nancy and Reed during their time of loss.

The couple was in for another devastating event in their lives when they discovered that Nancy was diagnosed with breast can-cer. Seemed so unfair that their friends was hit with such a double blow, but like when they lost their baby, they stuck by them like true friends should.

Nancy put up a brave fight but lost her battle with the disease five years later. With no child and no wife, Reed was left devastated. It was then that Reed needed Ellis the most. Ellis tried to support his friend but was left stunned when Reed decided to relocate to another city.

Ellis tried to keep constant contact with his friend for support, but it became hard with the distance between them, and there was always the shadow of Reed's gambling addiction. Ellis knew that was a constant obstacle in their marriage, but in many ways, Nancy had been the factor that kept Reed in check.

After few years, Reed seemed to make a comeback and made his move back to the city and started his employ at the center. Though they weren't as tight as they once were, they talked occasionally, par-ticularly when Reed was in need of Ellis's brand of deduction skills.

When they suffered the tragedy of losing Grant, Reed returned the favor and lent his support for both Dana and Ellis in the months that followed. And when their marriage crumbled over the grief of losing their son and eventually ended with divorce, he remained neu-tral and a source of friendship to them both. He felt he owed it to Nancy to keep their fellowship intact.

But through it all, there was the problem of Reed's gambling. It was something that Ellis rarely brought up because he knew how much it angered him when people asked him about it. Because their friendship wasn't as strong as it once was, Ellis had no idea the extent of Reed's gambling debts. He knew what desperation could do to a person but exploiting young people?

Ellis could still not believe that Reed could be driven to do that. What had become of his old friend?

After a brief pause, Ellis's thoughts shifted to Nahshon. He thought about the story he'd told him about how the previous foster parent used him for sports gambling. Something about the show of force in the intrusion into his home suggested that bigger forces were at play.

The more Nahshon comes to the realization of his abilities, the stronger they're going to be, which in the wrong hands can result in catastrophic results. He needed to find his young friend, and he needed to do it quickly.

Ellis sat back on the couch again after pacing around while biting on his thumbnail, an involuntary expression when pondering something. He tried to tap into his analytical mind to figure what Reed's next move would be. No one knew Reed like he did, and he knew his former friend to be nobody's fool. What he did was career ending and an arrestable crime, so whatever his intentions are, it was for all or nothing.

Suddenly, beside him on the coffee table, there was a buzzing coming from his cell phone. He slowly glanced over at it to see an unrecognizable number. Now was not the time to be bothered by telemarketers or solicitors, so he ignored it until it stopped. As he was about to recoil back in the seat, the phone buzzed again. Frustrated, Ellis grabbed the phone to personally give the caller a piece of his mind.

"Listen, now is not the time to be calling asking—"

"Ellis? Ellis! It's Nahshon!"

"*Nahshon!* Where are you? Are you safe?"

"Yeah! I was able to escape. But they're after me, and I don't know what to do!" Nahshon replied in a panic.

"Okay. I'm here with you. Where are you calling me from?"

"I'm at the telephones in the parking lot of a Shur Goal gas station. It's off the expressway, and there are a lot of trucks parked here," Nahshon responded.

"Is the parking lot you're at populated?"

"Yes. There's a lot of truckers hanging out around here."

"Good. Stay close around them and occasionally go inside the gas station. The more visible the people around you, the less chance that Reed and his company will try to go after you if they spot you."

"I understand. I gotta be honest with you, Ellis. I'm terrified of what they'll do to me if they find me. One more thing, I used my abilities to escape from their car trunk. I think they're getting stronger," Nahshon added.

"The important thing is that you are safe. You could tell me more about it later. There's much we got to discuss. But for right now, I got to get to where you're at."

Ellis took a deep sigh.

"I have to find a way to get to you. They took my keys and sliced my tires. They really pulled out the stops to make sure I couldn't follow you, Nahshon."

"What about my bike?"

"Your bike?"

"Yeah, when I came over your place. I put it to the side of your set of condos just to make sure that it was not going to be in anybody's view. I didn't want anyone to take it," Nahshon replied.

"Did you have your keys on you?" Ellis asked.

"No. I usually tape it underneath the dash panel so that I don't misplace it," answered Nahshon.

Ellis took the phone and walked outside his condo. He strolled over to the side of the building to find Nahshon's motorcycle wedged in between the garbage bin and his shed. He placed his fingers underneath the dashboard, and just as he was informed, the keys were taped underneath. Ellis put the phone back up to his ear.

"I'm coming, son. Remember what I said and stay around as many people as you can until I get there," he said as he got off the phone and rushed back into his place.

Nahshon was on the other end as Ellis got off. He slowly placed the phone receiver up against his chest.

"'Son,'" he whispered to himself as he reflected on Ellis's parting word before hanging up the phone.

As Ellis rushed back into the house, he brainstormed what he would need in his rescue of Nahshon. He got his jacket, grabbed some sunglasses to wear, and then went into his ring box and slipped one on his finger. Next he went to his lockbox and pressed a combination to open it and grabbed his pistol that he used for home protection.

He returned to the living room and took a second to glance all around, reflecting at all that took place earlier. He shook his head in disbelief and proceeded to rush out the door.

CHAPTER 15

Nahshon's eyes scanned slowly across the pictures of the magazine that he was holding, trying to calmly look oblivious to the person off in the distance staring at him. There was an uneasy stare that he was receiving, the kind that comes about from profiling. Nahshon's eyes shifted slowly and caught the woman at the counter almost as if staring through him. He rolled his eyes in slight frustration at the woman's efforts to constantly keep a watch on him.

Nahshon continued to ignore her during the moments she watched him as he occasionally limped around the store. He limped outside and sat out in the lot between groups of truck drivers conversing with each other at the truck stop rest point. He rubbed his ankle intensely as he wondered what kind of damage he did to it in his escape of the trunk.

The pain in his foot became too much to bear as he continued walking in and out of the store, so Nahshon decided to remain in the store and out of anyone's view. Once his limping worsened, the clerk decided to approach him. As she approached, Nahshon saw her coming and braced himself for whatever harassment she was going to give him.

"Honey, is there anything I can do for you?"

"I don't know what you mean," Nahshon responded gruffly.

"You been limping around here for a while, and it's not getting better. Anyone can see that."

Nahshon was taken aback by the lady's sincerity. Being a young man of color and being approached by an older white female was a scenario that he was never comfortable with being in. It usually didn't end well due to the sign of the times. The expression on his face softened as he realized the genuineness of the lady's concern. A greenish aura began to fill up around the woman's presence, and Nahshon began to feel at ease.

"I'm sorry. I hurt my foot, and I'm waiting for my mentor to come pick me up," Nahshon responded in a much calmer tone.

"I understand. You can stay in here on one condition: you grab yourself a big ol' fountain drink and *sit down*. You need to stay off that foot!"

Nahshon could sense the motherliness in how she spoke. It was a tone that he vaguely remembered from his mother and longed for all his life.

"Yes, ma'am," he responded.

"Good. Now while you're doing that, I think I remember the owner having foot surgery almost two years ago, and he may have a pair of crutches in his back office. I'll go back there and check," she responded as she made her exit into the back room.

Nahshon eased himself at the sound of the lady's generous words. He relaxed himself in the seat of the clerks behind the counter. As he drew a breath for relief, he heard the sound of a motorbike and lift his head up. It was Ellis who burst through the double doors and looked around frantically for his young friend.

"Nahshon? Nahshon! Are you all right? Let me look at you, boy," Ellis said as he embraced Nahshon.

He touched the back of Nahshon's head and then coursed his hands along his face. Then he intensely patted Nahshon down to check if he was hurt in any way. It was something parental that Nahshon thought Ellis would do if he was his late son, Grant.

"Ellis. I'm okay, calm down," Nahshon responded as he assured Ellis he was fine. "I think I did something to my foot though when I was escaping. I can barely walk on it."

Ellis looked down at Nahshon's foot. He started to formulate a plan for getting them out of there to safety.

"Ellis, the clerk here, she's been really good to me. She went back in her office to see about grabbing a pair of crutches for me to use. She should be back in a minute."

"Nahshon, I'm not sure we have a minute," Ellis said with a sense of nervousness.

Just then, the window of the front of the store shattered behind the two as shots rang out. Ellis grabbed Nahshon by the back and fell with him down to the floor. The clerk had returned from the back room, unable to find crutches, and as soon she entered the storefront, a stray bullet pierced her in her side.

Nahshon witnessed in horror as the woman who was so eager to help him was shot, and the gunshots continued to ring. He looked at a shaky display rack close by the doorway near the woman. With the speed of thought, Nahshon made reddish variables appear beside the rack. The numbers began to skyrocket, resulting in the display rack falling over in front of the injured woman. The display rack created a makeshift barricade of safety for the woman as a bullet struck a piece of the surface, possibly preventing it from striking the lady.

"Ellis, she's been shot! We got to help her!" yelled Nahshon as shots continued to be heard.

The two crawled over to the woman while staying low enough to not be in view of the shooter outside. They lifted the display rack over the woman as Ellis examined her wound. The injury was a flesh wound to her side with no sign of the bullet. Ellis signaled to Nahshon to find something to help stop the bleeding.

Meanwhile, once the shots began to ring out outside, people began to scatter. As people ran toward their vehicles for cover, some of the loitering truck drivers who were close enough to the own trucks reached in their vehicles to get their own firearms. They returned fire at Reed's accomplices, resulting in an impromptu gunfight.

These were cross-country drivers, familiar with life on the road and the perils that appear in that way of life. Not only were most of them gun owners, but they were quite proficient with them. The two men hunting for Nahshon soon found themselves outgunned and outmatched.

The men cowered behind their SUV as bullets riddled the outer side. The positioning they parked at once served as an advantageous perch, but now became the only reason for their survival and a means for a possible escape.

As bullets continued to hail, one of the men received a shot in the arm that ripped the fabric in his dark suit. He let out a sudden grunt as his partner looked on. It was only a graze, but it was a sure sign that they were overwhelmed and were fighting a losing battle. They looked at each other as they straightened their sunglasses and quickly crawled back into the SUV to speed away. The target would have to wait another day.

Meanwhile, inside the store, Ellis and Nahshon continued attending to the injured woman. Nahshon was applying pressure to stop the bleeding on woman's side while Ellis talked on the phone with emergency dispatchers. Most of the up-close shooting had stopped and the sound of distant random shots were scarcely heard in the faint distance, so their attention was more on the bleeding shop clerk.

Suddenly there was the sound of police sirens outside of the store as two officers cautiously announced themselves as they entered the store. Upon entering, the first sight was of the old white woman on the ground while the two men were draped over her. Both officers reached toward their guns and aimed them at Ellis and Nahshon.

"Police! Freeze!" they yelled as they sternly fixed their pistols on the perceived assailants.

Ellis and Nahshon looked up to see the officers pointing their guns at them as tension ripped into the air. Ellis eased away from the woman while Nahshon remained close to her, applying pressure to her gunshot wound.

"Back away from the lady now," one of the officers yelled.

"Sir, this lady has been struck by the gunfire outside. Let us help her. Please!" Ellis pleaded.

"Back away and get on the ground now," screamed one of the officers.

The other one was steadily aiming his gun directly at Nahshon. Ellis spotted this and eased his way in between the line of sight from the officer's gun to protect Nahshon.

"Please! Don't shoot him! He's only trying to help!" Ellis yelled back to the officers.

"H-he's only tr-trying to help," muttered the injured store clerk as she struggled not to go into shock.

As the exchange was taking place, Nahshon stayed fixed on the officer that was pointing the gun at him. Fear gripped him tight as he stared at the chamber of the gun. He could see red auras surrounding both officers. The one threatening him was a deeper shade of red. It was clear to Nahshon that the officer had deadly intent.

"Sir, if you do not move out the way, I will spray you!" the unarmed officer said as he pulled out a can of pepper spray from his side harness.

"I will, but please tell your partner not to shoot my friend!" yelled Ellis as he pleaded with the officer.

"Sir, I am not going to ask you again, *get on the ground!*"

"Not if he keeps that gun on that kid!" Ellis replied as he took a step toward the officer.

The officer sprayed in the direction of Ellis's face. He could feel the chemicals attack the edges of his pupils as the sensation of flame engulfed the surface of his eyes. The sudden burning caused Ellis to drop down to his knees and scream in pain as he labored to rub his eyes with his shirt.

The sight of seeing his friend and mentor, Ellis, dropped to his knees caused Nahshon to stand up. As Nahshon got to his feet, the armed officer nervously changed his stance toward the young man, Nahshon could feel the man's deadly intent toward him.

As he stared intensely at the chamber of the armed officer's gun, variables began to appear around the gun and skyrocket in value. It was a deeper different shade of red and more intense than that of the aura surrounding the officer. In what seemed like an instant as Nahshon got up, the officer fired his weapon, but the bullet became jammed in the chamber and exploded in his hand.

The officer shrieked at the intense pain of the jammed gun exploding in his hand as blood profusely flowed from his hand to the floor. He gripped his hand tight, not yet noticing two fingers that were badly damaged in his hand.

Nahshon rushed over to the blinded Ellis and held on to him. He watched as the officer that pepper sprayed Ellis immediately rushed to the aid of his injured partner.

"Ellis! Talk to me, are you all right?" Nahshon said.

"He blinded me. I can't see! My eyes are burning!" Ellis yelled back.

"You two run! Get out of here!" said the clerk as she held her side, appearing to be more attentive than when she was first shot.

The two looked in the direction of the injured store clerk as she nudged her head at them, signaling toward the hallway leading to the back.

"Side door to the right, pathway toward the back. Take it. It'll lead you outside to get away," she added.

The unarmed officer was too busy trying to help his wounded partner to keep his attention on Ellis and Nahshon. As Nahshon led Ellis toward the hallway with him, he turned around to look at the old woman. Gritting her teeth through the pain, she gave the pair a smile. "I'll be okay. Here!"

The clerk tossed Nahshon a pair of sunglasses that lay close to her that were originally on the rack that he made fall in front of her as a shield. Nahshon thanked her as he caught the glasses in his hand and continued to lead Ellis through the hallway to the sideway exit door.

As the two stepped outside the store on the unpopulated side of the building, Nahshon noticed the exit was not far from his motorbike, which Ellis had driven there. He led Ellis to the bike and sat him in front and then sat on the seat behind him.

"Nahshon, what are you doing? I can't see!"

"Then I'll act as your eyes for you," Nahshon replied.

"*What!*"

"Ellis, I can't press on the pedal with this foot, but you can hit the gas on the bike, and I'll guide you."

"Nahshon, this is crazy. We got to flee from those shooters!" Ellis said.

"Ellis, do you trust me?"

It was the same type of leap of faith that Ellis had asked of Nahshon. He calmed himself and then gave a deep breath as he gathered his composure.

"Yeah, Nahshon. I trust you," answered Ellis.

Nahshon closed his eyes and cleared his mind and reached out to the area around him. As he opened his eyes, the world around him was in a different perception as various tinges of red and green lay around him. It became clear to him that he was starting to embrace his abilities and use them at will.

"Okay, let's go," he said to Ellis.

Ellis wrapped his hands around the handlebars of Nahshon's bike and slammed his foot down the pedal to get it going. Nahshon grabbed ahold of his shirt with each hand and held on as the two took off. As their motorcycle exited the lot of the gas station, additional police backup was arriving and passed by them. Ellis nervously leaned back to receive Nahshon's instruction.

"What should I do now?" Ellis said. "Which way should I turn?"

"You're fine. Ellis, just keep going straight. I'll let you know when the turn," Nahshon replied.

Nahshon chose to divert most of his attention toward the green images in his sight as he perceived it to be the best direction for them to go. He made a conscious decision to use it as an impromptu map for their escape route. Ellis followed Nahshon's every vocal lead.

Unfortunately, one of those red images that his mind chose to not pay attention to was the car of the two accomplices of Reed's that had already escaped the shootout at the store parking lot. They were waiting at a red stoplight when they noticed the motorcycle pass by across their lane. They looked at each other and made a quick right turn to give chase.

CHAPTER 16

Reed sat back in the driver's seat of his car. He could still hear the sound of the engine powering down from the point where he parked. He stared at himself in the rearview mirror with a small level of disgust as he contemplated everything that had led him to that point.

He looked over into the cushion of the passenger seat and glanced at the stun gun sitting beside him. With his right hand, he felt the edges of the handle and coursed his fingers slowly along until he cautiously stopped at its business end and pulled his finger away, intrigued and yet terrified at the same time of the stun gun's potency.

Still lost in thought, Reed turned his attention to his left hand as he stared at the wedding band loosely dangling from his ring finger. With his right hand, he started to play around with the ring, sliding it gingerly back and forth along his ring finger as he kept his head down low and began speaking to himself.

"Nanc, I know you're ashamed of me. I wish I could blame my habits on your passing, but I know I can't. You always told me my addictions would be my downfall. But this…I have truly began lying in bed with criminals, and the actions I've taken are so irreversible, Nanc. And worst of all, I got Ellis entangled with my mess as well. I know that would've upset you more than anything. After everything we went through and he and Dana went through, you'd think our supporting each other would continue to this day, but the fact is, I'm the one that ended that. The people that I'm working for can destroy me, Nancy, and everything I tried to do in your memory."

Reed paused and gave a frail sigh and continued speaking with his voice now trembling from his sudden weeping.

"No. I'm the one who destroyed everything. I'm the one who fed that gambling addiction and used all our money and your foundation's money to try to cover up for my debts. I did that. No one else did. I created this mess. They're just threatening to expose it. I'm already tossing away my career and reputation with this, but your foundation, our home, your legacy is just too much. If I accomplish what they want from me, they will pay to fix everything including keep your foundation going on without me. So I can't say no to that. You know the real me would never endanger a child like I'm about to do this boy. Nancy, forgive me for what I've done and for what I'm about to do..."

Reed took the wedding band and slipped it from his hand back into his pants pocket, as if the ring symbolized the last bit of humanity he had left. He lifted his head back up again and looked directly at himself in the rearview mirror.

"You know what you gotta do. And this is the only way to do it," Reed said to himself.

He wiped the tears from his eyes and with newfound sternness, exited out of his car and locked the door using his key fob. He turned around to face the path leading toward the medical clinic where his late wife's closest friend, Dana Geniro, was currently working inside. He marched his way toward the entrance of the building.

As Reed approached the front desk, he evoked a worried expression of urgency across his face. The registration clerk at the desk looked his way with a smile customary for greeting.

"Good morning, sir. How can we help you?"

"I need to speak with Dana Geniro. I am a family friend, and there's been an emergency with one of her family members."

"Well, sir, she's in one of the offices right now with a doctor and patient. I could dictate a message to give her once the appointment is over," said the lady at the desk.

"Ma'am, you don't understand. There's been a serious accident with one of her family members. I am a trusted family friend and was sent to get her attention because she could not be reached," responded Reed.

He assumed that Dana was like most nurses who liked to conserve their phone's power by having it off at different times of the day. He leaned in closer to the desk with his fingertips pressed up against the front counter, further accentuating the urgency of his plea.

"Miss, I am a doctor myself. I understand your rules and procedures which you have to abide by. But this is a matter of dire urgency. I cannot tell you myself what it is, but I do need to tell Dana so that she can attend to it. If you understand what I mean...," Reed added as he extracted his facility ID badge from his pocket and quickly flashed it to let her know that his credentials were true.

Reed's gambit paid off as the clerk took a second to reflect on the meaning in his words. She pushed back on her rolling chair to stand up and faced eye to eye with Reed.

"I'll be right back," she said as she made her way to the back offices to alert Dana.

Reed stood confident in his accomplishment of his deceit, but he remained composed as he noticed the other office clerks sitting there watching him. He paced himself away from the reception desk and toward the patient door leading to the back offices to give himself time to prepare his ruse once Dana arrived.

As the door opened in the waiting room, Dana stepped forward, marching out with the lady from the clerk's desk close behind her. There was a look of nervousness and concern on her face. Reed could see it and mirrored his expressions to match hers as well.

"Reed, what's going on? I spoke with my brother Adrian this morning and—"

Read quickly grabbed her with both hands by her shoulders and pulled her aside away from her curious coworkers.

"Dana, you're the only one that can help. I'm here because of Ellis."

"Ellis? Listen, Reed, I can't continue to be go through this with—"

"Dana, I found a note. Ellis has done something to himself!" Reed responded as his whispered voice grew louder.

"What!" a startled Dana replied.

"Dana, listen. I found a note in Ellis's office. I don't know if it's the relationship between you guys or him still coping with the death of Gee. Somethings pushed him over the edge, and he's either going to or has already done something to himself."

"Where is this note at, Reed?" Dana questioned.

"The note? Geez, I must have left it in his office. Once I discovered it, I was so terrified. I read it then I rushed out, and it probably fell on the floor," Reed explained.

"We need to call the police, Reed!" Dana responded frantically.

"I did. They're en route to his apartment to do a wellness check. But I know him, Dana, and I don't think he's there. I do know a place that he had told me he goes to clear his head, and I'm assuming he went there. That's why I need you to come with me to find him. Because if there's a chance left that he hasn't done anything to himself, he will listen to you," Reed pleaded convincingly.

Without hesitation or a second thought, Dana nodded her head in agreement. Excluding her feelings on the state of their involvement, Dana offered to go get her coat. As she rushed to the back of the office, Reed stood there and tried to shift his gaze away from the prying eyes of Dana's coworkers, nervous that one of them would detect his deception by his suspicious body language.

"I'm ready," Dana said to Reed.

Reed led the way as they stepped out of the exit doors of the facility medical office and strode down the driveway toward his car across the street. Dana paused and stopped in her stride and looked up at Reed.

"Reed, why don't we take my car?" Dana asked.

"No!" Reed abruptly interjected. "It's just I feel more comfortable taking my car, that's all."

Dana accepted his response and continued to let him lead the way. As she glanced at Reed, she could see that he was cautiously looking around the area as they walked.

"Reed, why are you looking around so much?" she asked.

"Ellis is still one of my closest friends Dana, I don't want him to lose his job over all of this. People talk," Reed replied, feigning concern.

Dana felt relieved by Reed's statement and continued to follow his lead to his car. As they walked around the car to the sidewalk side of the street, Reed used his key fob to unlock the car's doors. Then he quickly approached Dana, obscuring her view of the contents he had inside.

"Dana, do you mind getting in the back seat? I have a lot of crap in the front passenger seat."

"No, not at all," Dana replied as she halted her steps to get into the front passenger side.

Reed opened the door to the rear passenger seat for Dana to enter and stood back, allowing her to sit her way in. As she lowered her head and began to enter into the back seat area, Reed pulled out a stun gun and ignited it against the back of her skull, shocking her instantly into unconsciousness.

He pushed the rest of her limp body along the rear seat of the car, making sure to completely have her in before slamming the door shut. Reed looked around quickly to assess if anyone in the vicinity saw what just took place, and when he was confident that the coast was clear, he rushed into the driver's seat of the car.

Reed sped off in his car and drove down a couple blocks until he saw a familiar underground parking lot area that was vacant and pulled in. He exited the car and went immediately to open the back-seat, where he looked upon a still unconscious Dana. He reached into his pocket and pulled out a pair of zip ties, which he then proceeded to bound Dana by her arms and legs with. He could hear her moan as he tightened the zip ties and gagged her. The sound of her helplessness saddened him.

Once he returned himself back to his driver's seat, Reed once again looked at himself in his overhead mirror. His eyes began to tear up as he reflected on what he did.

"I'm so sorry, Nancy," he said to the eyes in the mirror. "I did this for you."

Just then his cell phone began to ring, and he reached over into the area between the seats to grab it.

"Yeah? What is it?" he said to the person on the other end of the phone.

The voice on the other end of the phone began to talk, and Reed's facial expressions began to change as he listened on to what was being said. After the brief message was given, the voice on the other end of the phone clicked off.

Reed silently and slowly placed the phone back down in the space between his seats. He sat there for a few seconds as a slow eruption began to rip throughout his body.

"Damn it! Damn it! Damn it!" he yelled as he violently began punching the dashboard in a fit of blind, desperate rage.

He began breathing heavily, almost as if he was hyperventilating, and struggled to calm himself down. Once he accomplished numbing himself, he reached back over to grab his phone again and scrolled through his list of contacts.

As his eyes scanned over the list of names in his contacts, they finally paused to the name of the person that he needed to call next. It was the contact number for Ellis Daniels. Reed took himself a deep breath, and as the phone began to ring, he prepared himself to speak.

"Hello?" said Ellis's voice on the other end of the phone.

"You couldn't just stay out of the way, could you, Ellis," said Reed.

He sat there in the parked car and continued his conversation with the man whose former wife was kidnapped and lying unconscious behind him.

CHAPTER 17

Ellis could still feel the heat of the chemicals of the pepper spray stirring away at his corneas as he kept his head down low. He held a viselike grip on the handlebars of the motorcycle, terrified that one slip of his hand would cost them their balance and make the two violently crash. Never could he imagine that he would ever be bold enough to ride a motorcycle virtually blind.

For a few seconds, Nahshon closes his eyes tight and whispered to himself, "I can't accept anything harming me and Ellis on this motorcycle." As his eyelids began to open, the entire world around him was blanketed in the color of red aura, with occasional blotches of green appearing suddenly. This was his mind guiding him which way to go.

"Take a sharp right turn on this next street…now!"

Ellis followed Nahshon's lead and sharply turned the motorcycle onto the adjacent street. He quickly returned the steering to its straight formation as he clutched on even tighter to the handlebars. Suddenly there was a quick spark along the chassis of the bike, followed by a loud ping.

"What was that!" yelled Ellis.

Nahshon turned his head to look back. It was Reed's accomplices following them down the road. The accomplice in the passenger seat was halfway out the window, firing at them.

"It's the guys that shot at us at the gas station. They're back and chasing after us. One of them has a gun!" Nahshon yelled back to Ellis.

"What! We gotta find a way to shake them loose from us," replied Ellis.

Another shot rang out, but it was nowhere close to the bike. The screams of frantic people fleeing along the streets could be heard in the distance.

"Nahshon, focus on this word: *direction*."

Nahshon played the word over and over in his mind, and as he looked out at the green blotches of guidance, the blotchy shape of the green aura began to manifest as arrows, like the kind on a street sign. The new image of direction made it easier for Nahshon to navigate.

Back in the pursuing car, the accomplice firing the gun inched back into the passenger seat so that his partner could make the car go faster. It was obvious, with the swerving and control of the vehicle, that the driver was very experienced with pursuit.

The pain in Ellis's eyes started to weaken as he tried to open and focus his sight, but everything was still blurry. He could barely make out passing flashes, or what he perceived as possibly cars along the road.

"Get ready for sharp left, Ellis. We're going into an alley."

"Okay," replied Ellis.

"Now!" Nahshon yelled.

Ellis responded with a quick turn of the motorcycle into the alley. The sudden turn threw the pursuing car off as it flew past, leaving the two henchmen baffled. They looked ahead at the alley that the pair had vanished into and realized the car would not fit, so they elected to go around the block and try to catch them at the other end.

Down the narrow passage of the alley they sped as brick and metal along the sides zoomed past them. Everything in Ellis's vision remained a blur, and during one of the bumps along the pavement, his sunglasses fell off and shattered on the ground.

"Ellis, I'm seeing a green arrow directing us to make a sharp right as we exit the alley. It's very bright and blinking. I don't know what that means," Nahshon said.

"Maybe there's a probability field telling you that is urgent that I make this turn. Tell me when!" responded Ellis.

"Okay...*Now!*"

Ellis followed on cue and forcibly turned the handlebars all the way to the right as they exited the alley. The car with Reed's accomplices were heading straight toward them in an attempt to ram them as they exited from that end. The sudden turn caused only the rear of the bike to be clipped by the pursuers' car as another driver came forward from a different direction and rammed into them, causing their car to spin about in the street.

"Jesus, that was close!" Nahshon yelled.

"What happened?" asked Ellis.

"They tried to hit us as we got back on the street, but another car hit them. That's what it was trying to tell me. Aagh!" Nahshon yelled out.

"Nahshon, what's wrong? Ellis inquired.

"My head is starting to pound. Aagh," whimpered Nahshon.

"I was afraid of this happening. You're overexerting yourself, Nahshon. We gotta find a way to escape them."

Nahshon directed Ellis toward the road leading out of the business district. Suddenly out of nowhere, their pursuers' car barreled out from behind a building and kept the chase going. The henchmen in the passenger seat took another opportunity to try to shoot at the two. This time the bullet struck the dirt road beside them. Nahshon looked in the horizon and saw a wooded area up ahead.

"Ellis, I got an idea. Going to try to lose them in the woods," said Nahshon.

"The woods? What!"

"Trust me, Ellis. The aura leading to the woods is green," Nahshon replied.

"Then let's go," Ellis replied, trying to mask his nervousness as his vision was slowly returning.

Nahshon directed Ellis into the wooded area. As soon as they entered, there was a drop that almost made the entire bike fall over. The car with Reed's accomplices entered as well and fell down the same drop when entering the woods. It made the car turn sideways as the driver struggled to control it.

The motorcycle zoomed through different trees as Nahshon barked directions for Ellis to turn the motorcycle nearly avoid a collision.

"Right."

"Right."

"Left."

"Right."

"Left."

Ellis followed obediently. He could feel the bark of the various trees they passed flashing past them. Their pursuers were trying to follow them as best they could, but their maneuvering was leaving them behind.

The driver continued pressing the car beyond its maneuverable limits and came before a large tree stump that rammed against the bumper of the front of the car. The impact of the blow made the car overturn and slide down toward an embankment.

"We did it!" Nahshon celebrated.

Just then Nahshon's ability to see the aura around him started to fade as he reached his physical limitations. The exertion that he used caused him to become lightheaded.

"Ugh," he said as he collapsed against Ellis's back.

Fortunately, most of Ellis's vision had returned, and he was able to reach back and grab the pair of glasses off Nahshon and put it over his eyes in time to completely take over driving the motorcycle.

"I got you, son. Relax," Ellis assured him as they made their exit out of the wooded area.

Back inside the thick of the woods, Reed's two accomplices slithered their way out of the overturned car. The crash had injured the henchmen who had shot at Ellis and Nahshon. He regained his composure while assessing the extent of his broken arm. The other henchman, who was the driver, also composed himself and surveyed the area around him in the woods.

He then reached in his pocket and pulled out his cell phone and dialed a number on it as he calmly wiped the blood that was streaming from his nostril down to his face.

"Yeah?"

"Mr. Richardson, the target and his associate have both escaped. Our car is overturned in the woods, and we both have suffered injuries. We will need some time to before attempting recapture."

Meanwhile, Ellis drove himself and Nahshon farther down the road about a mile and pulled over into a well-populated playground area. He took a moment to collect himself and settle his nerves and then checked on his friend, who was slumped over against his back.

"Nahshon! Are you all right?"

"Yeah, I'm okay. I'm just exhausted, man. I just need a moment to rest," Nahshon replied.

"Okay, buddy. You stay there and relax. I'm going to stretch my legs a little," said Ellis.

Ellis took a couple steps away from the bike and Nahshon and paced around, pondering what their next move would be. Just then his cell phone began to ring, and as he looked at the caller ID, it said, "Reed Richardson."

"Hello?" Ellis said.

"You couldn't just stay out of the way, could you, Ellis?" said Reed.

"Reed, this has gone too far," Ellis replied.

"Oh no, it's about the go way further, Ellis. I have Dana."

Gripping dread came over Ellis as Reed's words resonated into his ears. Harm had come to the woman that he still was in love with.

"You sonofabitch," Ellis said coldly.

"Now you listen to me. Because of your meddling, you're going to have to follow exactly what I tell you or Dana here dies. You and that freak will come to the cliff overlooking the mountainside of Woodland Heights. You know, the place where we were heading with him until he made his little escape? I need him back there, Ellis, along with you. You will meet us up there and exchange him for Dana," Reed explained.

"Reed," Ellis said sadly.

"Any attempt to alert anyone or bring any kind of help and she dies, Ellis. These people are not playing. They *will* kill her...brutally."

"Who *are* these people, Reed?"

"You have an hour or Dana dies," Reed forcefully replied.

Ellis lowered the phone slightly as he glanced over at Nahshon, who sat up on the motorcycle soothing his injured foot and resting himself. Ellis then put the phone back up to his ear.

"One more thing: after the exchange, I cannot guarantee you will survive this. I'm sorry," Reed said as he followed up by clicking off his end of the phone call.

Ellis looked again at Nahshon while he put his phone back in his pocket. He began to step toward his young friend to tell him the grave news of what was in store for the both of them in about an hour.

CHAPTER 18

Carefree children frolicked around the park area as they took part in the enjoyment of the sunny summer day. The boys were tossing around the football as they ran about, trying to tackle one another, playing touch football. A group of little girls and their instructor were practicing with drill team routines. Other children occupied their time on swings and going down slides. In the distance from it all sat Ellis and Nahshon on a park bench.

"...and that's what Reed said before he hung up," Ellis said as he concluded sharing with Nahshon the phone call he had with Reed.

"I'm in a catch-22. Saving Dana means sacrificing you and, according to Reed, myself as well. Dana never asked for this, and I have no idea what they plan to do with you and your abilities. In the wrong hands, there could be—"

"I'll do it," Nahshon interrupted.

"What?"

"I'll offer myself to go freely with them in exchange for you and your ex-wife to be allowed to safely leave," Nahshon added.

"Nahshon, no," Ellis softly lamented.

"I never knew my father, Ellis. And the men that were in my life were nothing but users and abusers. For the last nine months, you have cared for me with more compassion and warmth than anyone in my life. I know I can never replace your son, Grant, but I feel like a son when I'm around you. And I can't let them harm you and your ex-wife. Grant never would...," Nahshon replied.

Ellis was overcome with emotion. He stood up in front of where Nahshon sat and leaned down, his head gently against the top of Nahshon's head, and wrapped his arm around his shoulder in a hug.

"Nahshon, you've just begun to tap into your abilities. Your power is expanding, the limits of which no one can say. Whoever is behind all of this knows this and probably intends to use you as some kind of weapon. Whatever they do with you, their end goal will be to use you up and eliminate you, because you will be too dangerous a threat. I can't let that be your fate, Nahshon. "I can't," Ellis added as his voice cracked while his forehead was still brushed up against Nahshon's.

"It's okay, Ellis," Nahshon replied as he placed his hand on Ellis's shoulder. "It's like what my mother said, '*I'm the ruler of my destiny,*'" Nahshon sung softly in a lighthearted jest as he placed his other hand on Ellis's shoulder.

"Your mother," Ellis replied as he reflected.

The poise and maturity that Ellis saw in the young man was almost overwhelming. His eyes began to water as he contemplated his young friend's sacrifice.

"Now let's go save your wife!" Nahshon said with a feigned sense of confidence.

Ellis and Nahshon both stood up from the park bench, and Ellis helped Nahshon along to get on his motorcycle. Ellis got on in front of him and started the motorcycles engine. He put the only pair of sunglasses that they had on as Nahshon leaned his head down, and the two sped off to head to Reed's rendezvous point.

The air was brisk and breezy, and a slight whistle could be heard through the wind as Reed stood still. His comb-over that he had worked so hard to disguise to people of his imminent balding rustled about. Normally this would be cause for him to frantically keep it in place, terrified of the discovery by others, but at that moment, it meant very little.

Flanked around him were the two henchmen that were through his ordeal for most of the day, along with two more men that arrived by another car sent by the company. With four sets of eyes on the situation, Reed felt confident that despite Nahshon's unpredictable abilities, there would be enough of a presence to make sure his acquisition would go smoothly.

As Ellis and Nahshon approached the rendezvous point along the cliff, they could see that additional help had been brought in from their secret protagonists. An extra vehicle was parked along with the already bullet-riddled vehicle of the first two henchmen. Ellis made sure to slow the bike down at a safe enough distance from his ex-wife's captors.

Ellis released the kickstand of the bike and slowly climbed off it. He then reached over and helped Nahshon, still prone to the use of one leg, off the bike as well. Nahshon directed his arm around Ellis's shoulder to help him stand up. The opposing entities were fixed on each other, reminiscent of a climactic gunfight in an old Western ghost town.

"Ellis!" Reed yelled. His voice carried along through the backdrop of the wind.

"Reed! Let me see her! Now!" Ellis yelled back in anger.

"It's all right. Go ahead and bring her out please," Reed said to the two men that had been accompanying him.

They went into the back of the bullet-riddled vehicle and released the trunk, this time by untying the thick rope that held it in place due to Nahshon's previous escape. They reached in and pulled out the bound and tied woman, who, despite looking a little disheveled in appearance, was in decent condition.

The sight of Dana being okay relieved Ellis and lowered his anxiety. When they removed the blinders from Dana's eyes, the glare of the sun blinded her. As her eyes quickly adjusted, she could see Ellis in the distance.

"Ellis? What is happening here? Who are these people? Why is Reed doing this?" she yelled out to him.

"It's going to be all right. We're going to do what Reed and his people say and we can go home," Ellis assured her.

"Ellis is right, Dana. If he gives us what we need, you can both go home safely," Reed added.

"Reed, I don't understand any of this. What's happened to you?"

"I'm sorry, Dana, there's no turning back for me now. The things I've done, the things I'm about to do, I can't ever go back to the life I've known."

Dana looked over at the suited men accompanying Reed. As she viewed each of his accomplices, she noticed one seemed particularly fidgety and anxious with his hand on the trigger of his gun, as if their conversation was beginning to annoy him.

"Shame on you, Reed. Nancy would be so disappointed in you," Dana said scoldingly at Reed.

The disgusted way in which Dana spoke to him left Reed rocked to his core. He turned himself away from Dana's sight and begin to walk over toward Nahshon. Ellis saw Reed making his approach and attempted to intercept him before reaching Nahshon. One of the henchmen pointed his gun and fired at Ellis, striking him in his arm.

The sensation of hot metal seared through his flesh as the bullet struck Ellis, entering between his lower arm and exiting out of his elbow. The burning sensation remained after the bullet exited, and a complete feeling of numbness came over Ellis as he realized he could not bend his arm. He clutched his arm while a commanding amount of pain set in as he looked up at his assailant and then at Nahshon. The initial shock began to set in as he became aware he'd been shot.

"Ellis!" Nahshon and Dana yelled out in unison.

The henchmen who had shot Ellis set his aim at Dana and was preparing to shoot her if she advanced.

"*No!*" screamed Reed. "You don't have to do this!"

"These two are not a part of our orders," said the stone-like individual.

"I-I know, but it was agreed on that these two could be released as long as we secured the target. We got him, so please let us stick with the original agreement and let these two go. They cannot get in the way now. Please," Reed pleaded with the henchman holding the gun.

The shooter took a moment to assess the situation as well as the validity of Reed's plea, still switching his aim between Ellis and Dana. He signaled to his partners to go ahead and grab Nahshon and bring him over for transport. Another one of the henchmen took out his walkie-talkie and spoke into it.

Despite having a gun aimed at her, Dana bravely ran over to Ellis to comfort him as he held his arm, still in shock at his injury.

"Send the transport in twenty minutes. Subject will be ready for pickup," another one of the henchmen said to walkie-talkie that he pulled from his side belt.

The henchmen with the walkie-talkie then walked over to Nahshon and forcefully grabbed the back of his neck in a viselike grip. He pulled Nahshon along with him as he walked past Reed.

"Come on. The chopper will be here soon for us," he said to Reed in passing.

As Dana was holding him tightly, Ellis looked up to see the henchman manhandling Nahshon as they walked closer to the area of the cliff. Without fear of getting shot again, Ellis leaped up from his crouched position and lunged forward to protect Nahshon from his assailants.

As Ellis started to run to the aid of his young friend, the henchman with the gun followed his movement, preparing to fire another time and take him down. Reed turned around to see the man about to shoot Ellis.

"*No! Wait!*" Reed yelled.

Nahshon also turned around to the sight of the man about to shoot Ellis. And in Nahshon's perception, time came halting to a stop as the environment around them cascaded with variables of numbers. As he looked beyond the shooter, he felt the variables guide his attention to another object around them—a fly. With the speed of thought, Nahshon asked himself what the chances of the fly buzzing in the ear of the gunman were.

With that task being given to himself, his mind began to manipulate the numeric variables around the fly and the ear of the henchman. The numbers shot upward in a reddish hue, and almost as if being commanded, the fly buzzed directly into the inner ear of the assailant, causing him to violently jerk his arm away from the line of sight of his target.

His finger pulled the trigger, and the gun went off, first striking the ground not far from his own foot. As he recoiled, his finger, still on trigger, pulled again, releasing another bullet. The bullet went through the opening between the tire of the second SUV and its frame, striking its gas line. It created a spark which infused with the leaking fuel and cause an ignition underneath the car. Flames could be seen jetting from underneath the vehicle as Ellis ran over to protect Dana while everyone else looked at the car in disbelief.

No longer able to contain the heat of the ignition, the gas pump erupted in an explosion, causing the entire vehicle to blow up like a bomb. Everyone and everything in the vicinity was struck by the blast, including the original bullet-riddled SUV, which was blown over by the shock wave of the explosion.

The explosion on the cliff could be heard and seen for miles, including the small-town area located down from the mountain range, containing the gas station where the shootout had taken place. As the boom of the explosion passed, the area was blanketed in smoke, metal, and fiery fluid.

CHAPTER 19

The billowing smoke saturating the area left over from the burning wreckage filled Ellis's lungs as he started to regain consciousness. When the vehicle exploded, he instinctively covered Dana as a shield, an act of loving sacrifice. He lifted himself from on top of her to look and see if she was still breathing. As his hand rubbed along her face, he could hear faint moans from her, and he was filled with relief that she was alive but still unconscious. His thoughts then turned to the condition of Nahshon.

Ellis ventured forth through the billowing cascade of smoke and flames from the exploding vehicles. Massive amounts of fuel were set ablaze on the ground as flames were everywhere, obscuring his vision as he slowly surveyed the area. He clutched his arm tightly to try to stop the bleeding from his arm due to the gunshot. As he stepped through the smoke, he saw one of the henchmen lying dead on the ground close to some ignited fuel. The flames got closer and closer to the man's body, so Ellis looked away, not wishing to see the sight of the person burning.

On another side of the cliff, he could see another henchman lying face down, barely moving but still alive. The last sight that he'd seen before the explosion was Reed close to Nahshon, so his focus was on finding one of the two. Slowly moving ahead, he could see the grisly sight of another henchman lying dead from a piece of shrapnel from one of the vehicles. The metal was lodged deep between his chest and collarbone. He recognized the face as one of the two original henchmen that assaulted him, and he showed little concern over his death.

He saw Reed coughing violently on the ground close to Nahshon's bike, which was up against one of the destroyed cars. The bike was leaking fuel as well, but Ellis paid little attention to it as he was trying to find his friend.

"Reed, where is Nahshon?" Ellis asked.

"Over there by the car," Reed replied as he struggled to gasp for air.

Ellis glanced over the side of the burnt-up SUV and saw Nahshon on the ground as he was trying to sit himself up. He made his way to his young friend and grabbed his shoulder, pulling him close.

"Nahshon, thank God you're alive. I gotta get you out of here!"

"Your wife. Is she okay?" Nahshon asked.

"She's gonna be fine. Come on," Ellis replied.

As Reed began to sit himself up and gather his bearings, he looked at Ellis and Nahshon talking. His attention became diverted to the sight of flames following along the trail of the fluid coming from Nahshon's abandoned bike, which was on the other side of them against the SUV.

"Look out!" Reed yelled.

But it was too late. The flames reached the motorcycle and caused it to explode, creating a blast that pushed the bullet-riddled SUV toward the edge of the cliff with Ellis and Nahshon in front of it.

The SUV came to a complete stop, nearly hanging over the ledge of the cliff while both Nahshon and Ellis were catapulted over the edge of the cliff. Ellis reached out to grab hold of the hand of Nahshon, who preceded him in the fall, while extending his other hand to grip on a piece of the bumper still attached to the bullet-riddled SUV on the edge of the cliff.

As Nahshon's fall temporarily got stopped by latching on to the hand of Ellis, the sudden jerk caused a pull in the already injured arm that made a sickening sound. Ellis released a horrifying scream at the enormous amount of pain as he clung to both the vehicle and to Nahshon.

Nahshon dangled in the air. His wrist was being held tight by Ellis's hand. He instinctively used both his hands to wrap around Ellis's for reinforcement. As he looked up, he could see Ellis's arm being stretched to its limit. A ghastly sound could be heard from Ellis in his agony.

Fibers of sinew and flesh began to tear. Bone began to crack along the fault lines created by the impact of the gunshot. The reality was that Ellis's lower arm was tearing away from his elbow. Ellis's other hand, which was gripped tightly around the SUVs bumper began bleeding from the sharp metal of the bumper cutting into the flesh of his hand.

The immeasurable amount of pain was beginning to put Ellis into shock, but he knew if he succumbed and passed out, he would release his grip on Nahshon, and he would plummet to his death. Ellis willed himself to stay awake and continue enduring the agony of having his limb ripped apart.

"Ellis! I'm too heavy for your arm to hold. It is tearing apart! Let me go and save yourself for Dana. If you keep holding on to me, either the bumper or your arm will rip off, and the both of us will die. I don't want that. I never knew my dad, but you've been more to me than any father I can imagine. They want me. If I die, then they have no reason to go after you and Dana anymore. Please let me go," Nahshon said as both his hands let go, only leaving the grip that Ellis had on his wrist.

"Nooooooo," Ellis painfully replied. "We had purpose... When I was a young grad student, I went to an off-campus bank to pick up my financial aid check that had just arrived. While walking around the corner from the bank, I passed a beautiful girl walking her little boy, and we exchanged glances at each other.

"I was so taken in by her beauty that I turned my head around for a second look and noticed a bus from the next block going through a red light and heading towards her and the boy. I ran back towards the girl to stop her from crossing the street and go into the path of the bus, but I was too late.

"That beautiful girl lost her life that morning, but I was able to grab hold of her young son and pull him back in time. I held that blood-soaked little boy against my leg as other people around me gathered to see if he was all right.

"All those years ago. Nahshon, it was *you*. I couldn't let go of you then, and I can't let go of you now," Ellis said in a mixture of pain and tears.

It all made sense to Nahshon now. Why, despite every encounter with the people in his life, Ellis was the only person that he ever met that always had a green aura around him. Since their first encounter, he always had a calming effect around Ellis, almost a yielding feeling, as if he knew without knowing that Ellis was there to help.

Nahshon's mind allowed itself to show him the memory of his walk with his mother. Gone were the blocks and restrictions that his subconscious had erected for his own protection. He placed himself back into the view of the young child walking along with his mother. As he looked up, he was greeted by the visage of his beautiful mother looking down and smiling at him as they walked. He could hear his mother's lullaby echo slowly in his mind:

> I'm the ruler of my destiny
> If I fall then it's because of me

Nahshon began to feel energy around him crackle as he looked up, transfixed on the plight of Ellis. He began to breathe heavily as the energy that was around him expanded out into the surrounding air. Reality around him began to flicker as if there was a tampering in its operation.

> *There is nobody who's got the power*
> *To determine what becomes of me*

As he reached out with his mind, he could feel all the ambient numbers around him. There was no longer a feeling of fear and confusion. The numeric variables were something to embrace and to master. Despite all this and his obsessive panting, there was an air of confidence in the mastery of the energy around him.

> I'm aware of what we're here to do
> And, do is our only choice
> And if you like it'll be ME and YOU

As he looked up at Ellis, the light brown coloration of Nahshon's eyes became opaque with a slight glow. Ripples of invisible energy cascaded against the rock of the cliff, causing the surface of the rock formation to shake.

The composition of the rock began to shift as a piece of the rock formation began to grow outward by Ellis's dangling feet. Ellis felt the perch-like formation and quickly placed his feet upon it to lift himself and relieve the pull that was ripping his arm apart.

The strain on his mind was immense as Nahshon felt the taxing exertion to his limits, but his will was strong. Blood began to flow down from both of his nostrils as Nahshon let out a primal scream. Stronger waves of energy were released among the ambient numeric variables around him.

More rocky extensions began to take form along the mountainside at different points along the drop, making an almost rock-climbing formation. Nahshon noticed a ledge formed by his feet and instinctively grabbed a foothold to alleviate the strain on Ellis and hold himself up from dangling.

Both Nahshon and Ellis began to slowly lift themselves up on the newly formed footholds. The energy that Nahshon was expanding began to wane as the numeric values all around them began to flicker and dim.

The fatigue began taking over as the energy around Nahshon began to dissipate. All the numbers around him began to flicker out as if they were being erased. Nahshon grew lightheaded; he could feel himself slipping into unconsciousness.

Dana, who was kneeling close to Reed and sobbing, looked over and noticed by the car the sound of Ellis struggling to return to the surface. She got up and ran over to the other side of the car that was positioned at the edge.

"*Ellis!*" she yelled as she frantically ran to the aid of her former husband.

She grabbed hold of Ellis's back as she looked at the arm clutching the SUV's bumper. Blood was dripping from his fingers as the metal was cutting its way through from his firm grasp. Dana used her weight to pull Ellis up over the edge and saw to her horror the damage done to his other arm that was still holding on to Nahshon. She joined her hands with his to help pull them up and alleviate the strain to Ellis's arm.

As he emerged from the edge of the cliff, a wave of panic and realization overcame him as he became aware of his surroundings. He pulled himself and Nahshon farther away from the cliff's edge. Dana joined in pulling Ellis farther away from the edge of the cliff and closer to the other side of the SUV.

Dana crawled back and watched Ellis as he cradled the nearly unconscious Nahshon. It was at that moment that she could see once again the husband who loved their son, Grant, at all costs. She was touched by Ellis's devotion to the young man while at the same time saddened at the thought of her lost son.

"Nahshon, it's okay. I got you. We're safe now." Ellis said in a comforting tone. "Your power, it's..."

"It's gone. I used it up. I can't see or feel anything anymore, Ellis. For the first time, I feel nothing," Nahshon replied in a faint voice.

"It's all right, son. You saved us."

"We saved each oth..." Nahshon attempted to reply as he blacked out.

Ellis held the young man close as if he had found something that he once lost. He could feel Nahshon breathing and made the distinction that he was left unconscious from the phenomenal exertion of the power that he'd used. Ellis gently laid him on his back to rest.

"Ellis, you're all right. Good," said a familiar voice that made Ellis turn his head from looking at Nahshon.

It was Reed, who was barely propping himself up from the ground close by. Protruding from his abdomen was a large piece of shrapnel from the SUV that initially exploded. Reed's loss of blood was heavy, and he was sweaty and growing pale. Ellis and Dana ran toward him, and Ellis held him in his arms.

"Oh, Reed, no," Ellis said in a somber voice.

Ellis glanced upward toward Dana, who was an experienced nurse and had the expertise to determine the severity of such a wound. Dana looked at the angle of the shrapnel in Reed's abdomen as well as the look in his eyes and gave a melancholy nod back to Ellis. Reed was not going to make it.

Emerging on the scene were two of the henchmen recovering from the explosion and the sight of their fallen colleagues. They appeared battered and confused, not sure what to make of the scenario that was in front of them.

"Reed, hang in there. We're going to call for help," said Ellis, totally oblivious that the henchmen stood by not far from him.

"No. Please forgive me…the both of you," Reed uttered as tears flowed down his eyes as he looked at Ellis and Dana.

"Reed, save your strength. You—"

"Listen to me. You have no idea what's coming for you. There are forces, powerful forces that want the boy. And they won't stop, Ellis. They won't stop until he can—"

Suddenly, a distant shot could be heard, and Reed was cut short by a sniper's bullet going through the crown of his head. The brutality of the gunshot to Reed startled Ellis as he fell out of his arms. Blood sprayed on him as he quickly gathered his thoughts and looked to shield Dana from the sudden attack.

The two henchmen were also taken surprise by the sniper's attack and looked around for the possible assailant as they distanced themselves from Ellis and Dana and spread out to look around. The henchman with the walkie-talkie looked over at the neighboring mountain cliffs and raised his hand up to radio in the situation. Another shot rang out, and a bullet pierced through his skull, dropping him backward to the ground. Shocked at the sight of his fallen colleague, the other henchman turned to look out in the direction that he thought the shot came from and was also shot in the head by another sniper's bullet.

Ellis tried desperately to shield Dana with his body while trying to look around to see where the attack was coming from. Nahshon still lay unconscious and was too far for Ellis to reach. He quickly glanced for a second to see the bodies of the two henchmen as they lay on the ground.

On a distant mountain cliff, the sniper lay perched on his stomach. He was a man of average build and young, far too young to have such a level of skill at being a marksman. The line of sight from his viewfinder shifted from the remaining henchmen toward Ellis. As much as Ellis was trying to shield Dana's body from his attack, he left himself exposed, and the sniper had a clean shot at the back of Ellis's head.

His focus toward Ellis changed to Dana as he had a clear shot through his viewfinder at the unprotected side of her temple. His eyes looked away, taking away his focus from her, and then returned as he moved his line of fire from Ellis and Dana and toward the unconscious body of Nahshon. He returned his focus through the viewfinder as it narrowed in at a clear shot at the top of Nahshon's head. He drew a deep breath at his target and fixated on the shot for a second and then suddenly pulled away.

"Another time," he said confidently as he relaxed his hands from his rifle and placed it on the ground.

The sniper pulled himself up and stood staring off at his targets in the distance. He reached in the side pocket of the backpack that was strapped to him and took out a walkie-talkie like the model the henchman on the cliff had. He turned it on and pressed a couple of buttons before bringing it up to speak.

"Transport for recovery of one. The tracking module is on. I'll be ready at alternate location," the sniper said.

The sniper placed the walkie-talkie back in his backpack and proceeded to disassemble and pack up his sniper rifle and viewfinder. Once that was finished, he reached in his pocket for some facial tissue. He looked out once again at his previous targets on the distant cliff and proceeded to wipe some blood that had formed at the edge of his nose. He let out an enthused chuckle and proceeded to pack up equipment onto the parked motorbike he had arrived on and began to make his exit down the road from the mountain peak.

Minutes had passed since they were fired upon, and Ellis continued to try and shield him Dana from harm. Not sure if the sniper was still targeting them, Ellis theorized if the sniper wanted them dead, they would already be and that he'd probably had left, but being out in the open could not continue. Slowly, he began guiding Dana away from the body of Reed and toward the SUV by the cliff for possible cover.

As the two began to slowly crawl toward the SUV, they could see that Nahshon was starting to come to. They made a beeline for that direction and went to aid Nahshon as he remained on his back. Ellis got down and lifted Nahshon's head off from the ground as he finished opening his eyes.

"Ellis…what happened?"

"It's okay now. I got you," Ellis assured Nahshon.

Dana tore off some of her skirt and began to make a makeshift splint for Ellis's grotesquely mangled arm. He seemed unfazed as she placed his arm in the splint, his attention on the care of his exhausted friend.

Dana stood up and looked out into the sky and noticed the far-off semblance of a helicopter beyond the mountains. The helicopter was not coming their way; rather, it lowered itself and disappeared between a cluster of mountains. She kneeled back down to Ellis to get his cell phone from his pocket and stood back up to dial for emergency assistance. Within the hour, an ambulance along with the sheriff and fire department arrived on the scene.

CHAPTER 20

Eight months later

The pavement remained somewhat slick from the precipitation of rain that occurred earlier in the day. Nahshon tightly clutched the steering wheel with both hands, his arms locked straight out and tight. His eyes were wide open, taking in everything in the vicinity of this view as he glanced at the wetness of the road.

"Easy...loosen those arms on the wheel," said Ellis. "Breathe."

"I still think you should be the one doing the driving," replied Nahshon.

"Oh, don't worry. I will get enough of this road when I have to drive myself back. You have to learn to relax, Shon. You don't choose the road conditions to drive in. You learn to adapt to it. Besides, you're doing fine. You're focusing too much on the conditions of the road. Try focusing more on the signs overhead that you pass, and the rest will come naturally."

With Ellis's vote of confidence, Nahshon was able to relax himself more at the wheel. Ellis observed him, and a smile came across his face. Nahshon felt his mentor's support, and it encouraged him to remove his fear.

The last several months had brought monumental change. With Ellis's guidance, Nahshon was able to pass his GED just in time to apply for college out of state. The bond between the two had strengthened as well as Nahshon's rapport with Dana. With Dana's blessing, Ellis was able to invest in Nahshon's tuition with the college fund that he and Dana had saved to use for Grant.

"Now be sure you make your appointment next week. Remember, you got one more scheduled surgery left," Nahshon said in a parental tone.

"Oh, so now you're the one being the parent and telling me what to do?" Ellis responded with a chuckle.

"I'm just saying. Your memory might not be up to snuff."

"Ha! 'Up to snuff.'" Ellis scoffed at his notion. Let's see… Tomorrow morning, you have a 9:00 a.m. meeting scheduled with your RA in your dorm so that he can get to know you. At 10:00 a.m.: freshman orientation in the conference room on your student union building, which you will be attending. At noon, the student bookstore opens, so make sure to be there with the list of curriculum books that I went ahead and typed up for you. Around that time, your meal plan should be arriving to your room. If not, go to the administration office. It closes at 5:30 p.m.

"Around 6:00 p.m. your time. I will be expecting a call from you to fill me in on your first day's events and if there were any problems. That will leave you with a few hours in the evening to prepare for your first English lit class at ten o'clock the following morning."

Nahshon kept his poker face despite his amazement at Ellis's retention. He had grown used to his mentor's knack for detail.

"Fine, you got it all figured out. I just have to be there for it. Speaking of which…Ellis, I'm coming in as a freshman. Why do I have classes like statistics and probability in my workload. Don't you think I have enough on my plate with my schedule?"

"The classes on statistics and probability are going to aid your abilities in the long run, Nahshon. You'll have a better grasp should anything return."

"It's gone, Ellis. I can't feel anything anymore,"

"You don't know that, Nahshon. Give it some time."

They allowed themselves to reflect on Ellis's words. The car began to veer over the median line. Nahshon became alarmed and tightened his grip on the steering wheel. Ellis reached over across with his hand and tugged the steering wheel back into position, bringing the car back over and into correct alignment with the lane it was supposed to be in.

"I got you," Ellis said.

The two arrived at the airport parking area and found a spot close to the shuttle bus going to the main terminal. Once stopped, Nahshon made his way out the car first so that he could get his luggage out before Ellis even thought of making an attempt to go for his luggage. He knew his mentor well and didn't want him to make the mistake of trying to use his recovering arm.

"So what are your plans after you see me off?" Nahshon asked as he sat his luggage on the ground outside of the car.

"I'll probably be on the phone on the way back home. Dana wants me to give her a call. She wanted to make sure everything went well with sending you off. I think we are going out to dinner tonight. I have to figure out a new restaurant that we both can agree on," Ellis replied.

"I'm glad you and Ms. Dana are having another go at your relationship."

"Really it's just baby steps. We're trying to explore a fresh start. We miss Grant, but we also missed each other. So who knows, maybe this might work," said Ellis.

"I think it's great. The love is still there. You could see it after everything that we went through."

"We gotta move forward, Shon. I'd like to think that Reed's at peace now," Ellis said calmly as he readjusted the sling around his arm.

"Yeah," Nahshon replied as he listened. "The shuttle bus is coming."

The pair had made it to the terminal and through the security checkout along the way to the gate of Nahshon's flight. As they walked along the corridor, there was a feeling of anticipation taking over. Nahshon realized he and Ellis would soon part ways. He thought about how far he'd come and how Ellis had helped him to get there. Finally, he had someone in his life he could truly trust and know they would never leave him.

They stopped right in front of the gate where the last security check was before leading to the seating area for Nahshon's departing flight. Ellis reached into his sports jacket with his good arm and pulled out the departure boarding pass, which he handed to Nahshon.

"Well, this is far as I can go without catching a flight. All your boarding passes are here. You only have one layover in St. Louis. It is only twenty-seven minutes until your connecting flight departs. I looked at the airport layout online, and the connecting gate is close to the other side of the airport, so you're really gonna have to foot it to get there on time. So don't go strolling casually."

"Okay, okay," Nahshon replied as he chuckled. "I got it. No time to waste between flights."

"Yeah," Ellis said calmly. "I'm going to miss you, Shon."

"Ellis, I'm not leaving your life. I'm just going off to college. Besides, when the semester ends, I'm coming back to spend time with you and Ms. Dana."

"I know. I'm just being weird, I guess."

"No. I get it Ellis," Nahshon replied as he placed his hand on Ellis's shoulder. "I'll never be able to thank you enough for helping me get into college. It's like a dream come true."

"This was your mother's dream for you, Shon. All her hopes and dreams for you are for you to make happen. You're gonna make her so proud."

Ellis's words were soothing to Nahshon as he reflected on his late mother and the efforts that she'd made to one day have him at this moment.

"That reminds me. Shon, I want you to have this. When you get through the loose items scanner at the checkout, I want you to put this on," Ellis said.

Ellis reached in another pocket of his jacket with his arm and pulled out his old class ring attached to a chain and gently placed it in Nahshon's palm. It was the same ring that had helped trigger Nahshon's remembrance of his mother and Ellis.

"Oh, Ellis. No, I can't take this."

"You can. This ring was meant to be for you. Wherever you are and whatever you do, this ring will remind you that you're never alone."

Nahshon looked down in his palm at the ring and chain. He clenched his palm and felt the ring in his hand. It gave him peace of mind and left him speechless.

"Now get going," Ellis lightly directed Nahshon.

"Right," Nahshon confidently replied. He carefully embraced Ellis, being mindful of his arm and with his carry-on luggage in hand, began walking away toward the item security scanners in the distance.

Ellis sighed as he watched Nahshon walked away, imagining having the same feeling if he was seeing an adult version of his beloved Grant off to college. He gently smiled and turned around to walk away.

Nahshon passed through the security scan, and as he retrieved the tote on the conveyor belt containing his items, he looked out into the distance at Ellis walking away. He noticed Ellis making a beeline toward the nearest restroom, and as he entered, there were two men in suits around that area suspiciously following Ellis.

As the two strange men converged in front of the restroom to enter and confront Ellis, a motorized transport cart came out of nowhere and violently struck the two men, creating a dramatic scene around the area among airport travelers.

Airport security swiftly arrived and attempted to secure the area of the accident by sectioning it off from bystanders, while detaining and questioning the driver of the transport vehicle and the couple on it he was transporting.

The incident created a huge scene within the airport gate as people gathered around outside the enforced perimeter of the occurrence. Emergency medical personnel came on the scene to attend to the gravely injured men struck by the vehicle. One of the airport security officers went into the men's restroom to direct anyone inside to come out away from the scene.

Airport EMTs arrived to take the injured men from the airport to an ambulance waiting outside the airport located at the secluded exit away from the public. The two men who'd been seemingly going after Ellis were carefully being strapped onto the gurneys to be rolled away through the airport.

Nahshon nearly finished putting back on all his items including the necklace Ellis had given him. As he continued to watch the scene unfold in the distance, he could see a few men leaving the restroom, including Ellis, who was at first taken off guard by the scenario in front of him, but quickly followed the officer's instructions to move away from the scene.

Ellis cautiously made his way through the onlookers while occasionally looking back at the sight of the incident. Though he had a puzzled expression on his face, he nonetheless resolved to leave the airport and go on with his day as planned.

Nahshon distanced himself from the security check line and continued to watch Ellis as he walked out the corridor leading toward the outside of the airport. The conversation with him and Ellis would have to take place eventually, but for now he felt their lives deserved an inkling of normalcy, especially with his move to college and Ellis's upcoming surgery.

Nahshon watched as his friend disappeared outside the door of the airport. An opaque flicker came across the surface of his light brown eyes and then left. He smiled and reached down to grab the handle of his carry-on bag. He turned around and continued his walk toward the area where his flight would be departing in the distance.

As Nahshon walked, ambient numbers surrounded the area around him. No longer were they spotty-looking numeric values, but instead numeric percentages clear and concise and at his beck and call to command.

No longer was his power something to fear and dread, but something to explore and embrace. His power had returned, stronger and easier to control than ever.

As Nahshon continued walking in the distance, he began to whistle his childhood lullaby, his beloved mother's favorite song by Chaka Khan, surrounded by a sea of numeric percentages that only he could perceive and a clear and unwavering realization of what the possibilities for the future might hold and that he was the master of his fate.

Printed in the USA
CPSIA information can be obtained
at www.ICGtesting.com
JSHW080229010624
63653JS00007B/132/J

9 798890 612069